KATE KLISE

SCHOLASTIC INC.

New York Toronto London Auckland Sydney
Mexico City New Delhi Hong Kong Buenos Aires

This book was originally published in hardcover by Scholastic Press in 2006.

ISBN-13: 978-0-439-79448-0
ISBN-10: 0-439-79448-X

12 11 10 9 8 7 6 5 4 3 2 1   8 9 10 11 12 13/0

Printed in the U.S.A.   40

First Scholastic paperback printing, December 2008

The text was set in Adobe Garamond LT

Book design by Elizabeth B. Parisi

For my brother, James

Life can only be understood backwards;

but it must be lived forwards.

—Søren Kierkegaard

*   *   *

'Cause tramps like us, baby we were born to run.

—Bruce Springsteen

1.

The sheriff delivered the subpoena on my fourteenth birthday. At first, none of us knew what it meant. *Libel? Intent to malign?*

We were being sued because of a magazine article I'd written?

For almost a year after that, it felt like we were living in a kaleidoscope that kept turning, forcing us to change colors and shapes. Or like we were a top that someone started spinning, and then we just kept spinning faster and faster.

A TV talk show host once asked me: "When did you realize your family had become a household name?" In an attempt to be humble (because is there anything more awful than a fourteen-year-old kid whose family has become a household name?), I hemmed and hawed and finally said something stupid like: "Um, I'm not sure we're really that famous."

Of course we were famous. And I'll tell you exactly when I first knew. It was after my mom started homeschooling us again in Dallas. One day, she gave Ben and Laura a test on percents. The extra-credit question on the test was this:

```
If 86 percent of all children's T-shirts
worn in this country are Bargain
Bonanza-brand T-shirts, and 93 percent
of those Bargain Bonanza T-shirts are
from the NormalWear line of clothing,
what percentage of children's T-shirts
worn in this country has a picture of
our family on the tag? (Remember: 100
percent of NormalWear clothing has a
picture of our family on the tag.)
```

I'll spare you the calculation. It's 79.98 percent. (My mom would let you round that up to 80 percent.)

But you see my point. At one time, eight out of every ten children's T-shirts worn in the U.S. had a little tag in the back with the NormalWear trademark under a tiny silhouette of a family of seven, each the size of a hyphen, waving from a boat.

Our family. Our boat. Our world: a kaleidoscope turned by the hands of people who claimed they owned us.

2.

But I should back up. Because not many people know what happened in those first few years after we left Normal, Illinois.

If you saw *Normal*, the cheesy movie allegedly based on my family, you'll recall that my family fled Illinois after an ugly incident at the junior high school my sister Clara and I attended.

Long story short: Clara was running for president of her seventh-grade class. Her campaign consisted in covering the walls of Normal Junior High with her goofy (yet harmless) "VOTE CLARA HARRISONG for a POSITIVE WAY of THINKING!" posters. But then some popular kids, led by the awful Randy Breedlove, wrote hateful things (like *Poor White Trash*) on the posters, which Clara never should've seen because I should've stopped the kids or destroyed the posters. But I didn't because I couldn't, so she saw them.

And then the next thing you know, my family was leaving our yellow brick rental house in the middle of the night and moving to a houseboat in Alabama.

When we left Illinois, Clara was twelve years old. I was eleven. My brother Ben was eight. Laura was six, and Sally was just four years old.

The guy who directed *Normal* collapsed the two years we spent on the S.S. *O'Migosh* (that was the name of our houseboat) into three dialogue-free minutes at the end of the movie. During the closing credits, "we" (meaning the actors who portray us) gaze with dopey smiles at two turtle-doves leading the *O'Migosh* toward distant islands.

Not quite. For one thing, I never saw doves when we were on the houseboat. For another thing, living on a house-boat, especially one as old and rickety as the *O'Migosh,* was hard work. Something was always *always* breaking. Which wasn't as bad as it could've been, because my dad could fix anything. But not while we were on the water.

So our routine went something like this: Sail for a few days until something broke. Get nervous that we wouldn't make it to shore before the boat sank and we all drowned. Make it to shore. Set up tents in a campground or park. Camp out for a week or so while Dad fixed the boat and the rest of us hit the local yard sales and discount grocery stores. Return to the water in our repaired (for the moment) houseboat. Sail for a few days until something broke. Etc., etc., etc.

Sometimes we returned to shore for nonmechanical reasons, like when Mr. and Mrs. Fluff, our rabbits, and their son, Fluff Junior, all died within thirty-six hours of one another. We went ashore to give them a proper burial. In the eulogy, Clara said solemnly that she believed the Fluffs would always be part of our family, and that just as we had cared for them during their lives, the Fluffs would now take care of us. To which Ben replied: "Who wants a bunch of dead rabbits taking care of them?"

Was living on a houseboat fun? Well, sure. As fun as anything you do every day is fun. But it was our life, too. It wasn't a game. It wasn't a gimmick. Our lives were driven by basic needs: food, water, and shelter, with occasional holidays thrown in to separate us from the rest of the animal kingdom.

For our first Christmas on the houseboat, Dad suggested we dock at Sanibel Island, Florida, famous for its seashell-strewn beaches.

"We'll go shell hunting early on Christmas morning," Dad said. "Then we'll give the shells to one another later in the day. They'll be our gifts."

"Can we decorate our shells?" Laura asked.

"Good idea," Mom said. "Everybody decorate your shells."

So that's how we celebrated Christmas — by exchanging seashells. Clara's, of course, were mini-masterpieces: tiny portraits of us, painted on sand dollars. Dad used his cordless drill to make shell necklaces for the girls and Mom. For Ben and me, Dad made shell keychains. He promised to make us copies of the ignition key to the *O'Migosh*.

My artistic skills were still completely lame, so I wrapped my shells in holiday cards I made with notebook paper. While my brother and sisters ran up and down the beach, dodging gelatinous blobs of jellyfish and filling their curled T-shirts with shells, I struggled to think of simple but honest messages for everyone in my family. To my mother, I wrote:

> All my love to you, Mom,
> on this Christmas Day.

For Dad, I chose the words:

> Merry Christmas to a man who earns my
> respect and love each and every day.

I tried to pour so much feeling through my fingers and onto the paper, it was difficult to hold the pen steady. But I didn't get it right, judging from the reaction.

"Nice wrapping job, Charles," Dad said, discarding my note.

"It's not *wrapping paper*," Mom said. "It's a Christmas card. Right, honey?"

"Yeah," I said. "Or no. It's just . . . whatever you want it to be."

What I wanted to be was a writer. But the difference between the words in my mind and their cheap appearance on paper was always a surprise and a disappointment to me. I tried to write about love. I tried to write *love*. But I often ended up with something people misunderstood or threw away.

People throw away love all the time without even realizing it. It can be right there in front of them and they don't see it. They don't understand it, so they can't believe it.

What I'm saying is believe it, even if you don't understand it. Believe it *especially* if you don't understand it.

But now I'm really getting ahead of myself and this story.

3.

This is the story about one year of my life — from my fourteenth birthday to my fifteenth birthday. But to understand it, you have to know a little bit more about what happened before I turned fourteen, back when we were still living on our houseboat.

For two years, we lived on and off the S.S. *O'Migosh.* Even when we weren't broken down (mechanically, I mean), we still needed to spend some time on land so Dad could make money for groceries, boat stuff, and our yard sale purchases.

This wasn't hard for my dad. All he had to do was find the local building supply store and go there early in the morning, when contractors were coming in for supplies.

Mom found educational value even in this.

"If Dad goes to HomeLand every morning for ten days and gets a job every day but three, what's his success rate in finding work?" Mom asked Laura and Ben one late fall morning.

I was thirteen then. We were holding our homeschool classes at a park in Destin, Florida. Our desks were two picnic benches pushed together. Sally, Laura, and Ben sat at one bench, Clara and I at the other.

Ben, now ten years old, and Laura, eight, frustrated Mom by refusing to use anything resembling logic to solve what she called her "lamebrain teasers."

"I think it's . . . 50 percent," Ben said, peeling long strips of paint off the picnic bench.

"Wrong," Mom said. She was spreading generic peanut butter on hamburger buns. Our cold, wet laundry hung on a clothesline tied between two trees.

"Is it 200 percent?" Laura asked. "Or 250 percent?"

"Wrong and wrong," Mom said.

"You've got to at least tell us who's warmer," said Ben. "Me or Laura."

"There's no *warmer* in math," Mom said. "There's correct and incorrect. Right and wrong. And you're both 100 percent *wrong*."

"But I'm good, right?" interjected Sally, now six years old. "I'm *gooder* than Ben, anyway."

"Better," Mom said. "And don't chew on your hair."

My mother was such a wizard at math. I knew I'd inherited a bit of her knack for calculations. But Ben and Laura — and even Clara — always just guessed wildly, never bothering with the formulas Mom wrote carefully on index cards.

(Poor Mom. She even had all the cards laminated, thinking that might help. But it only confused my brother and sisters.)

"How can a negative times a negative equal a *positive?*" Laura demanded as she bit into her peanut-butter sandwich. "It just doesn't make sense. None of this makes sense."

"Yeah," said Ben, always up for an argument. "A negative times a negative *can't* equal a positive. Because remember what you said, Mom? About two wrongs not making a right?"

"Just because something's negative doesn't mean it's wrong," Mom said, exasperated.

"I don't *get* this!" Laura whined.

"Me neither," Ben said.

Clara tried to help. She was fourteen and working on a series of nature paintings on driftwood.

"Think about it, you guys," Clara said. "*Not* smoking or *not* killing someone. Those are negatives, right?"

"Yeah," Ben said. "Because you said *not.*"

"Right," said Clara. "They're negatives. But they're not wrong. *Not* killing someone isn't wrong."

Laura's eyes welled with tears. Ben just banged his head on the side of the picnic bench.

For this and other reasons, Ben decided that winter he wanted to return to school — or "school school," as he called it, to distinguish it from Mom's school. Because of this, Laura wanted to go to "school school," too. And because Laura wanted to go, Sally did as well.

After much discussion on the merits of Florida, Alabama, Mississippi, Texas, and even, briefly, Cuba, we decided to dock at Dauphin Island, Alabama, not far from where we'd started our "adventure," as Dad insisted on calling our house-boat experience. Someone at a building supply store told Dad he could get work with a crew building upscale homes in a new beachfront community.

Staying in one place would also give Dad a chance to make structural improvements to the *O'Migosh*.

"We'll put her in dry dock for a year," Dad explained. "I'll work on repairs in my free time. Make her shipshape for the next adventure."

We found a mobile home park near a public beach and rented an aqua double-wide trailer: #42 Starry Sky Cove.

After quizzing Ben and Laura on their multiplication

tables till Laura dropped the question mark at the end of her answers ("Say it like you *know* it," Mom said), and Ben could recite all but the twelve times tables with a yawn, Mom enrolled them and Sally at Judge Roy Bean School. They would begin classes the second week in January.

Clara refused to be enrolled as a second-semester high school freshman.

"Going to high school is just not who I *am*," she told Mom and Dad.

Our parents had made the strategic blunder of telling us they'd been hippies when they were young. They couldn't now deny Clara's request to be homeschooled, especially when she proposed a legitimate schedule. It included reading, math, painting, science experiments, and two chapters a day from the college-entrance exam prep books that Mom picked up for her at a used bookstore.

The PSAT study guides were a gentle hint to Clara that even though Mom and Dad were willing to negotiate on some things, they expected her — and all of us — to attend a four-year college.

"Nothing wrong with technical school or junior college," Dad often said, referring to his and Mom's educations. "But just think of all the things you could do with a *real* college degree."

I thought about college a lot. I imagined myself being discovered by a distinguished professor who would recognize my unique gifts and talents, pluck me from among my dimmer classmates, and launch me to stardom.

My unique gifts and talents? Hmn. I was still working on that. Though I wanted to be a writer, the only things I ever wrote were the deathly dull entries in my journal. I blamed my boring writing on two things:

1) My lackluster personality.

2) My bland reading habits, which those days consisted of rereading the collection of haunted house mysteries I'd brought with me from Normal.

I needed to start thinking a little bigger here.

To prepare myself for my bright (but still fuzzy) future, I followed Clara's lead and convinced my parents to let me design a homeschool curriculum more challenging than anything offered by the local junior high. I did, thanks to a stack of college textbooks I bought at a pawn shop for a dollar: *Introduction to Philosophy. Anthology of American Literature. Western Civilization (The Ancient World Through the 17th Century). Economic Theories and Practices.*

The philosophy book was my favorite. After I'd read the first three chapters, Mom told me to write a summary of what I'd learned.

"*Philosophy* comes from the Greek words *philo* (love) and *sophia* (wisdom)," I wrote. "So philosophy is the love of wisdom. It's about trying to make sense of yourself and the world around you."

"Is that all you've learned, sweetheart?" Mom asked when she gave my paper back.

It was. The thing is, I thought it was pretty cool. Until then, I'd always thought I was just a worrier. Turns out other people had been worrying for centuries about the same things I worried about, like whether or not there's a God, and if there is, where is He when you need Him? And other things, like: *Am I the person I think I am? If not, who in the world am I, anyway?*

The difference was my fellow worriers didn't call themselves freaks or geeks or poor white trash. They called themselves *philosophers*.

While Mom walked my younger brother and sisters to their first day of school, I sat at the picnic bench outside our trailer and read Chapter Four, *Know Thyself*. It seemed like a good thing for a thirteen-year-old to know.

As a kid, I'd always had a clear sense of who I was. Back in Normal, I was the unpopular kid in class. I would've been the invisible kid, too, had it not been for the time in fifth grade when I was reading *The Yearling* in class and started crying.

(Okay, so that was another reason I was reluctant to enroll in eighth grade in Alabama. Word gets around on this stuff.)

I needed a new and improved self. But what? *Who?* Those years on the *O'Migosh* had complicated things for me. Living on the water and looking up at that big night sky could make you feel the world was huge and full of possibilities. You could be anybody you wanted to be!

Or could you? That same sky could also make a person feel small and vaguely hopeless.

Mostly I felt torn between the two extremes, which made me feel stuck. Paralyzed. Like that day in Normal when those popular kids were writing nasty words on Clara's campaign posters and I just stood there like an idiot, unable to stop them.

So, I balanced my grandiose fantasies about my future successful self with a more humble prayer I sent up nightly from the pull-out couch in the trailer. The prayer went something like this:

Dear God, who am I supposed to be? What's the plan? I want to be prepared. And if it's not too much trouble, I'd like to be wonderful and unusual in some small way. Please. Thank You. Amen.

Sometimes I'd add a P.S. to my prayer:

If being wonderful in a big way is available, I'll take that, too. I'm thirteen years old, God. I'm ready to feel extraordinary.

4.

Laura loved third grade and claimed to be the smartest girl in her class. She said her teacher, Mrs. Driscoll, was The Number One Nicest Lady In The Whole Wide World.

Dinner in our trailer became a nightly tribute to *real* school. The fun science projects. The teacher's aide in Sally's first-grade class, who gave her a headband to wear during art class and then Let Sally Keep The Headband For Good. The free breakfasts ("Mom, you've just *got* to learn how to make French toasties!") and lunches.

Sally even enjoyed her weekly visits to the school's speech therapist, who worked with Sally on her *Rs*, which still sounded like *Ws*. Every night before bed, Sally recited a litany of phrases — *The rapid rabbit was rabid. Run, rabbit, run* — designed to strengthen her *R* muscle.

Ben struggled academically. ("I might be able to get five or six, but no way no how am I going to remember *thirteen*

17

colonies.") But he thrived socially, making a dozen friends within his first week of fifth grade at Judge Roy Bean School, known locally as The Beanery.

Ben's best friend was a classmate named Dylan Goodman, whose family lived in Sunset on the Water, the fancy beach-front community where Dad was working that winter. Most Saturdays, Dad walked Ben to Dylan's house and then proceeded to the jobsite.

If it wasn't too cold, I tagged along. The house where Dad was working had a private beach behind it, with built-in umbrellas. It was perfect for reading.

Ben (being Ben) didn't flinch when Dad, clad in his coveralls, greeted Dylan's mother, who was often still wearing her bathrobe. Dad didn't seem to mind the contrast either. Sometimes he even accepted Mrs. Goodman's offer to have a cup of coffee in the solarium, a sunny room with curved, floor-to-ceiling windows overlooking the Gulf of Mexico.

"Now that's what I call rich," Dad told me one Saturday as he and I left the Goodmans' sprawling house. "Drinking coffee in your robe at nine o'clock in the morning."

Dylan had an older brother named Walker, who was fourteen. One Saturday in late February, when Dad and I were dropping Ben off at Dylan's house, Mrs. Goodman invited me to stay, too.

"Walker's putting together a scale model of the Colosseum," Mrs. Goodman said. "Why don't you stay and help? It looks like fun."

I tried to send Dad an S.O.S. with my eyes, but he was looking at Mrs. Goodman in her fleecy robe. Her curly blond hair was pulled up in a loose, movie-star bun. I guess she was sort of pretty — for a mom.

"I've seen those kits," Dad said. "Historically accurate and all that, right?"

"Exactly," said Mrs. Goodman. "It was a Christmas gift from my brother. He's an architect in London."

I had no desire to stay. I wanted to read *Introduction to Philosophy* in peace on the beach, as I'd planned.

"I'll be back around four," Dad said, ignoring my eye signals. "I'm building custom closet shelving for a lady attorney. The blouses you women own."

Mrs. Goodman laughed. Then she turned serious. "You build custom closet shelving?" she asked, one eyebrow arched comically.

"Yeah," Dad laughed. "Nothing easier."

Mrs. Goodman clasped her hands, prayerlike. "I want to redo my entire dressing room," she said. "Maybe you could look at it — after you finish whatever you're working on now."

"Sure," said Dad. "I'd be happy to." And then he left with a mug of hot coffee.

Mrs. Goodman delivered me to Walker's bedroom on the second floor.

"Walker, show Charles what you're working on," she said, standing in the doorway. "He's spending the day with us."

Walker looked at me with profound disinterest. "It's just . . . this thing," he grunted.

"Cool," I mumbled weakly. I instinctively turned my philosophy book facedown and held it firmly against my leg.

"Have fun!" Mrs. Goodman chirped as she left. It sounded like *Half fun*.

My eyes scanned the room, trying to take in all the electronics, clothes, hair products, and movie posters. (Were those autographs *real?*) I could hear Dylan's and Ben's explosive laughter in a distant room.

I sat on one of the twin beds for more than an hour, watching Walker snap pieces of white plastic together and talk on his cell phone.

"Not exactly *baby*sitting," he said into the phone. Then, turning to me, he asked: "How old are you?"

"Thirteen," I said. "And a half."

"Thirteen," he repeated into the phone, laughing. "Yeah, I know."

I stared at my Bargain Bonanza tennis shoes. I'd bought them for a dime the week before at a yard sale in our trailer park.

I hated the shoes. I hated Bargain Bonanza. I'd always hated that stupid discount store and the way it made me feel so inadequate.

I stood up to leave.

"Bye," I said.

"Whatever," said Walker.

I found a set of back stairs and started down them, hoping I wouldn't run into Mrs. Goodman. Instead, I walked directly into Mr. Goodman's study.

"Oh, sorry," I said, turning quickly.

"Hello," Mr. Goodman said, smiling at me from behind a large desk. "Ben's brother?"

"Yes," I said. "I'm Charles. Harrisong."

"Charles Goodman," he said. He extended his hand to shake mine.

He was wearing a blue silk bathrobe covered with yellow commas. My mind flashed to the haunted house mysteries I loved. Every mansion had a room exactly like this one, with dark wood furniture and walls lined with leather-bound books. The only thing missing was a raven sitting on a globe.

"Anyone ever call you *Charlie*?" he asked.

I cringed at the nickname I hated.

"Sometimes," I said.

"God, I hate when people call me that," Mr. Goodman said, pouring coffee from a sleek silver thermos into a mug. "It's just awful, don't you think? Like Charlie Brown. Please. Sit down."

I folded myself into a dark green leather chair while Mr. Goodman took a sip of coffee and swallowed loudly. He saw my book.

"Philosophy," he said. "I'm impressed."

He offered me coffee. I watched as he poured a navy blue mug full of the steaming brew and passed it to me across the desk. I drank a bitter mouthful, trying not to scowl.

Mr. Goodman showed me what he was reading: a catalog of telescopes.

"I'm determined to discover a new star," he said. "A completely different kind of star."

I looked at the antique telescope that stood next to his window.

"Try it," he said, following my eyes. "Please."

"I don't —"

"No, really," he said, standing up. "Go ahead. Have a look."

I positioned myself behind the telescope, not knowing

what to do with all the brass dials and knobs. I closed my left eye and peered through the tiny glass eyepiece with my right.

"Well?" he said, standing beside me. "See anything?"

All I saw was a gray and fuzzy blob. I remembered my frustration in fifth-grade science class when we studied the microscope. The only thing I ever saw magnified was my eyelash.

"No," I said, stepping away from the telescope. "I'm not very good at this stuff."

"Neither am I," he said. "You have to wait till it's dark to see the stars — though they're always there, of course."

He took a sip of coffee.

"Did you know years ago, sailors navigated by using the stars?" he asked. "No telescopes. Just their naked eye."

I thought of all the times we'd been lost on the *O'Migosh*. Mom had eventually bought a box of maps at a flea market in Biloxi. She labeled and stored them in jumbo Ziploc bags, but Dad never looked at them. It was one of the few ongoing arguments aboard the *O'Migosh:* Mom's desire to plan versus Dad's insistence that we go with the flow.

"We're intrinsically linked to the stars," Mr. Goodman said. He was walking around his study. "Everything you see, everyone you know, has the tiniest trace of ancient star debris. We're all literally stars. Isn't that something?"

"Yeah," I said, not quite following him.

Mr. Goodman and I looked through the telescope catalog. He told me about the various features on top-dollar equipment. My eyes kept drifting from the pictures of the telescopes to the prices at the bottom: *$14,900. $39,900. $129,900.*

How in the world did people afford this stuff?

Then Mr. Goodman pointed out all the cool things in his office. I liked how he could do this without being a show-off.

"This," he said, picking up a crusty old compass, "is something I stole off my brother's boat. And that's a picture of the time my wife forced me to wear a white tuxedo. I keep it only to remind myself never to wear a white tuxedo again. Black. Only black."

I asked Mr. Goodman what his job was. He told me he was the publisher (a publisher!) of a magazine called *Modern Times.* Before I knew what I was doing, I told him I wanted to be a writer.

"I'm not surprised," he said. "You look like a writer."

I'm sure I blushed.

"Are you working on anything?" he asked.

"You mean . . . *writing* anything?" I said.

"Yeah," he said. "What's your work-in-progress?"

I told him I kept a journal on and off.

"I've never been disciplined enough to keep a journal," he said.

Then I told him I'd been thinking of writing about my family and our experiences over the past few years. Truth is, I hadn't thought about it at all until I said it.

"Tell me more," he said. He seemed genuinely interested.

So I told him how we'd left Normal after the poster incident at school; how we'd bought the S.S. *O'Migosh* sight unseen; how we'd been living on it — and off it — until our recent move to the trailer.

Mr. Goodman listened to every word. He squinted, as if trying to remember something.

"Write it for me," he finally said, tapping his chin. "Write it all."

5.

So I spent the month of March writing.

I wrote about Boy Scout camp and Clara's campaign for class president. I wrote about the popular kids at Normal Junior High, including Randy Breedlove, whose claim to fame was that he'd gotten a girl at our school pregnant.

I wrote about how I was the only kid in my class who lived in a mustard yellow rental house that didn't have air-conditioning. I wrote about daydreaming in church, crying in fifth grade, and Mrs. Flanagan at the Normal Public Library. I even wrote about the way I used to hide from classmates when my mom took me on those dreaded shopping trips to Bargain Bonanza.

I wrote it all, just like Mr. Goodman told me to.

I called it a *paper,* still locked in the vocabulary of junior high. But Charles Goodman ("For God's sake, please call me *Charles*") said it was a *manuscript*. After he read it, he called me at the trailer and asked me to come over to his house on a Thursday afternoon.

"I'm not a very popular man today," he said, handing me a cup of hot tea with a fresh lemon wedge on the saucer. We were sitting in his study.

"Really?" I said. "Why?"

"I finished your manuscript last night, Charles."

"Oh," I said, suddenly loathing myself for sticking the stupid paper in his mailbox a few days earlier.

God, why am I such a loser? Why am I such a worthless, talentless, stupid —

"I am completely under its spell," he said. "I called my managing editor this morning and told him to scrap the May layout."

I still didn't get it.

"Charles," he said, "I'm going to run your story about your family's experiences in Normal and on the houseboat in *Modern Times*. It'll be the cover story for the May issue."

"Oh my gosh," I said.

I was dizzy with happiness. Not only was my secret fantasy coming true, it was happening ahead of schedule.

Thanks, God!

"I love the vulnerability and the rawness," Mr. Goodman said. "You have an interesting style, Charles, and a real flair for the dramatic."

He said the magazine would pay me $1,200.

"Wow," I said, almost breathless. "Can I get some copies when it comes out, for my mom and dad?"

Mr. Goodman laughed. "Of course. We'll get you a hundred copies. You'll be able to use this as your college admissions essay."

First, I used it as a Mother's Day gift. My parents couldn't believe when I presented Mom with a tissue paper-wrapped copy of the May issue of *Modern Times* with the cover story, "Our Life in Normal (And Why We Had to Go)," by Charles Harrisong. Nobody could believe it, especially the bit about the $1,200.

I got the check in July, shortly before my birthday. I cashed it at First Bank of Dauphin Island and asked the teller for twelve one-hundred-dollar bills.

I loved being rich! I loved being famous!

Well, okay. So I wasn't famous yet. But that was just around the corner. In the meantime, I loved thinking of all the things I could buy.

I decided to blow the entire $1,200 on presents — not for me, but for everyone in my family. And Charles

Goodman, too. I knew exactly what I'd get for him: a telescope for his study.

I was looking at a telescope catalog, smelling my birthday cake baking in our trailer's tiny oven, when the sheriff arrived at our aluminum door.

*   *   *

You would've thought it was a joke. If you were like me, you would've looked at my mom and dad staring at the forty-eight-page complaint the sheriff delivered ("That there's a *federal* lawsuit," he said helpfully), and given Laura credit for pulling off a decent prank for a change. This was much better than the *arrest warnts* she used to tape to the bathroom mirror back in Normal. (*"Ben, you're arrestid for disturbing the peace! Charles, you're arrestid because you are not the boss of ME."*)

But this had all the details you can never get right when you're trying to play a joke on someone. The crisp white paper. The sheriff (with a real gun!) coming to our trailer. The legal mumbo jumbo.

Dad was still working for the lady attorney. Her name was Bonnie Barker. She'd hired him to "do" all of the closets in her house. When Dad called her and told her about the lawsuit, she came over that night.

Dad and I were sitting at the picnic bench outside our

29

trailer when Bonnie pulled up in her gold convertible with the IMALWYR license plates. She was younger than I'd imagined. She looked like a college student in her Alabama State tank top.

Dad handed Bonnie the lawsuit and she thumbed through it, standing up. Mom brought out a tray with purple plastic tumblers and a pitcher of sun tea. She was wearing an ironed blouse and a jean skirt.

"This is ridiculous," Bonnie said, not glancing up from the legal papers. "Totally and absolutely ridiculous. Oh, thanks." She took a long swig of tea and sat on the edge of the picnic bench.

"Don't say anything until I get back," Mom yelled over her shoulder. She returned seconds later with one of Ben's half-used school notebooks and a pen. She opened to a blank page and wrote *Lawsuit* on the first line.

"Okay, go ahead," Mom said. She'd put on lipstick for this meeting.

"Look, you guys," Bonnie said, pulling her brown, shoulder-length hair into a ponytail. "I'm a real estate lawyer. I don't know crap about intellectual property law. But I know this much: With libel, you have to prove intent to malign. And were you *intending* to malign Bargain Bonanza in that magazine article?"

She pointed a finger, cocked like a gun, at me.

"No," I said. "I was just trying to write something that —"

"Back up," Dad interrupted. "What does *intent to malign* even mean?"

"The basic idea," said Bonnie, taking another gulp of tea, "is that Bargain Bonanza — or the attorneys for Bargain Bonanza, I should say — are claiming that Charles wanted to hurt Bargain Bonanza. They say they're experiencing a drop in sales" — she read from the lawsuit — " 'due to the mischaracterization of Bargain Bonanza in "Our Life in Normal (And Why We Had to Go)" as an unfriendly and uncaring retailer, and that this is exactly what author Charles Harrisong intended.' "

"That wasn't it at all," I said.

"It's crazy," Mom said.

"Nuts," added Dad. He pulled on a thread hanging from his cutoff shorts.

"Of course it is," said Bonnie. "And isn't Bargain Bonanza's whole deal that they're a place where the little guy can go to buy cheap clothes and stuff? And then they slap a lawsuit on the littlest guy around?"

She flipped to the first page of the lawsuit. "Well, technically it's not Charles they're suing, but you two, 'Frank and

Allison Harrisong, legal guardians of Charles Harrisong,'" Bonnie said. "The real question is: Why are they going after such small potatoes? No offense, but you don't have the kind of assets to make this worth their time."

"Can't get blood from a turnip," Dad said with a smile.

"Exactly," said Bonnie. "But they can get a judgment against you."

"A *judgment?*" said Mom, writing the word in her notebook.

"If they can prove Charles's magazine article really hurt sales, they could get a jury to award them a lot of money. Millions."

"Of *dollars?*" Mom asked. "But we can't pay that."

We sat in silence. It was starting to get dark. Clara had taken one of her nightly walks on the beach. Laura and Sally were squealing in the distance. They were eating pieces of my birthday cake from paper towels and watching Ben catch fireflies. He'd used a pencil to punch holes in the lid of a mayonnaise jar.

"I'm throwing these lightning bugs in the slammer," Ben yelled. "They're going *down*town."

"What should we do?" Dad finally asked quietly.

"If I were you?" said Bonnie. "I'd countersue. This is a

frivolous lawsuit. It's malicious prosecution. I'd countersue and ask for two million in punitive damages and then I'd —"

"We just want it to go away," Mom said. "What can we do to make them understand that Charles didn't mean any harm with what he wrote?"

"I really didn't," I said. My voice was quivering. I could feel my eyes getting wet.

"We know you didn't," Mom said.

"I could call the attorneys and ask them to meet with us and discuss some sort of settlement," Bonnie offered. She was undoing her ponytail and raking a hand through her sun-streaked hair. "At least then you could get these people across the table from you and talk to them."

"That sounds like a good plan," Mom said. Then she looked at me: "We'll celebrate your birthday another night, okay, honey?"

"I don't care," I mumbled. "It doesn't matter."

"It's your birthday?" Bonnie asked. "How old are you?"

"Fourteen," I said. *Too old to cry,* I thought.

"Well, happy birthday, kiddo."

After Bonnie left, I heard Mom and Dad agreeing not to discuss the lawsuit in front of the rest of the family.

"No need to worry everyone," Dad said.

The next morning, I walked to the Goodmans' house. A visibly nervous Mrs. Goodman escorted me to her husband's study and then made a hasty exit.

"Charles, I'm so sorry," Mr. Goodman said, standing up from behind his desk.

He proceeded to tell me about the release language on the back of the $1,200 check.

"I'm afraid it's standard practice," Mr. Goodman said. "By endorsing the check, you assumed all responsibility for everything you wrote. It's crazy, I know. And the worst of it is, the attorneys say I can't even talk to you about any of this. I'm so sorry, Charles. I never intended for this to happen."

I believed him. I really did. Then again, Charles Goodman never would've let this happen to one of his children. Apparently you couldn't get sued for being careless with other people's kids.

"I wish I could help," he said.

"Me too," I replied.

And then, because I couldn't think of anything else to say or do, I held out my hand and said, "Good luck with your star project."

As I was leaving, I passed Walker on the back stairs. He was going up as I was going down. When he got to the top of the staircase, he turned and said, "Hey, did you really get sued?"

"Yeah, I guess," I answered.

He looked down at me and smiled. Then, with almost reverence, he murmured, "That is *so* cool."

My first brush with fame. I confess I felt idiotically flattered.

6.

Three weeks later, after countless letters and phone calls between Bonnie and the attorneys at Bargain Bonanza's corporate headquarters in Dallas, a meeting date was set. Bonnie assured my parents they wouldn't have to pay a penny to the discount giant — or to her.

"You can build a deck off my guest bedroom," she told my dad.

Our position was simple, Bonnie said.

"We'll agree not to file a malicious prosecution suit against Bargain Bonanza if they'll withdraw their lawsuit against you. What we're saying to Bargain Bonanza is that their lawsuit is so ridiculous, we can sue *them* for filing it. But we won't — provided they drop it within fifteen days."

The meeting was scheduled for one o'clock at Paradise Found, a tropical-themed motel in downtown Dauphin Island. It was owned by one of Bonnie's clients.

"We've got the Seagulls in Flight banquet room till five o'clock," Bonnie said. "It won't take that long. Besides, I've got a real estate closing at four thirty."

To my surprise, Bonnie said I was expected to meet with the Bargain Bonanza lawyers, too.

"I want them to see what their fourteen-year-old villain looks like," Bonnie said.

My face must've registered distress, because she quickly added: "Charles, I want them to see what a good kid you are. Just wear a clean shirt and a pair of good pants. No jeans."

I liked Bonnie — mainly because she seemed to genuinely like my family. She told Mom and Dad to bring Clara, Ben, Laura, and Sally to the motel.

"I don't want them in the meeting," Bonnie said. "But they can use the pool. The Paradise Found has a brand-new pool with a curlicue sliding board. What's not to love there?"

*   *   *

My family didn't have a car. Bonnie was nice enough to offer to drive all of us to the meeting in shifts in her convertible, but Clara and I said we'd walk. It was three miles, which was fine with Clara. Taking long walks was her second-favorite thing to do, after painting.

"You know, Chums, this isn't your fault," she said as we

walked on the shoulder of Highway 2 toward downtown Dauphin Island.

"Oh, please," I mumbled gloomily. "It's completely my fault. One hundred percent my fault."

"You didn't mean for all this to happen," she said.

"Just because I didn't *mean* to screw up doesn't mean I didn't," I said.

Ever since the sheriff arrived at our trailer, my guilt had sat in my gut like a stone. If I hadn't told Charles Goodman I wanted to be a writer, none of this would've happened. Clearly I was guilty for getting my family into this legal mess.

But I felt guilty for other reasons, too. All the time I'd been spending with Charles Goodman was time I used to spend with Clara. She and I were always close when we lived in Normal. But we'd grown even closer since then. Most mornings, Clara and I worked on homeschool stuff. She had her *All You Need to Know to Ace the PSAT* workbook and I had my *Introduction to Philosophy*. In the afternoons, we'd find a shady place on the beach where she could paint and I could write boring stuff in my journal.

Charles Goodman changed that. Not that he ever asked me to choose between him and Clara. But I did.

I chose to spend time with him. And I chose not to show Clara my manuscript before it appeared in *Modern Times.*

"I should've let you see the article before it was published," I said as the tires of an eighteen-wheeler threw dust in our faces. Clara and I were still a mile from the motel. My freshly ironed shirt was already trashed.

"I wanted it to be a cool surprise for everyone," I continued. "But, ugh, I shouldn't have written all that stuff about Randy Breedlove and your campaign posters. I'm never writing again."

Clara and I walked in silence past a sign crediting the local chapter of the Audubon Society for maintaining the littered stretch of highway.

"It *was* a cool surprise," Clara finally said. "I didn't mind that you wrote it. I guess . . . well, I just sorta wish you'd asked first."

"What would you've said?"

"I would've said it was fine," she said. "Chums, you were always more upset by that stuff at school than I was. I don't *dwell* on the past like you do."

"Then why —"

"Let's just see what happens," she said.

Then she punched me in the arm: "You will so write again."

*   *   *

Lawrence Leech and Alan Grayson were the Bargain Bonanza attorneys. Leech looked older than my mom and dad —maybe fifty years old. He was strong and beefy, with bright white teeth and red horn-rim glasses. It was impossible to look at Lawrence Leech in his dark blue suit and not think of an American flag. He was in charge of Bargain Bonanza's "brand identity."

Alan Grayson was even older than Leech. He was tall and thin, but his lips and eyelids were flabby. Grayson was Bargain Bonanza's trademark attorney.

Both Leech and Grayson stood up when Bonnie, Dad, Mom, and I walked in the Seagulls in Flight banquet room. The adults shook hands. We took our seats on opposite sides of the conference table.

Bonnie thanked the attorneys for coming from Dallas to meet with us. Then she began outlining our position. She called the lawsuit "not only laughable, but frivolous and actionable." She talked about the public relations nightmare Bargain Bonanza would face if they pursued this lawsuit.

"And finally," Bonnie said, "if you *do* proceed with this litigation and my clients are forced to file a malicious

40

prosecution suit against Bargain Bonanza, I will also file whatever paperwork is necessary with the Texas Bar Association to begin disbarment proceedings for you, Mr. Grayson, and you, Mr. Leech."

"*Reeeeealllly?*" Alan Grayson said. "And I thought you asked us here to try to mediate a settlement in this case. Not to initiate a second lawsuit."

"My clients don't want to file a lawsuit," Bonnie said, her face turning red. "But we will if you don't withdraw your complaint within fifteen days. Or, look, if you need thirty days, we'll give you that."

Lawrence Leech took over. With a gentle, singsongy voice, he began to speak in words and phrases so foreign to me, I wasn't sure which were nouns and which were verbs.

"And *Bargain Bonanza versus Lou Katz* is completely on point, as is the *Thompkins* case, where the defendant so grossly maligned our brand identity. . . . Of course trademark law is unequivocal on the rights of trademark holders to —"

Grayson was interrupting. "With our satellite accounting division, we can prove actual damages to the penny," he said. "And if you've read the ruling in *Bargain Bonanza versus Johnston,* you know that we don't have to prove *deliberate* intent to malign. The Fifth Circuit has practically written the book on the new standard of proof, which is whether, in fact, harm was done, regardless of intent."

"Exactly," said Leech. "What difference does a person's *intent* make? Case in point: *Bargain Bonanza versus The State of Wyoming.*"

My mind was a blur. *This,* I thought, *is what Mom's word problems must sound like to Laura and Ben.*

"What it boils down to," Grayson said, "is the piracy of our brand identity. Piracy, pure and simple."

Piracy? They were accusing us of being pirates?

From where I sat at the end of the conference table, I could see a corner of the motel pool and the occasional flash of my brother and sisters in their brightly colored bathing suits. They looked like darting, exotic fish.

At three o'clock, we took a break.

"They're jerks," Bonnie said as she, my parents, and I walked around the Paradise Found parking lot. "But I'm in over my head. You need an intellectual property attorney. Personally, I think those guys are full of it. But they're threatening to make an example of you. Frank, they could garnish everything you earn for the rest of eternity. They're pit bulls about protecting Bargain Bonanza's billion-dollar brand identity."

"Brand identity?" asked Dad. "I'm not even sure what that means."

"Their image," said Bonnie. "Who they are — or pretend to be. They want people to think the best of Bargain Bonanza so they can sell more crap. Let's just try to keep them talking so I can figure out where they're coming from."

She looked at her watch. "Yeow. I've gotta be out of here in an hour."

Ten minutes later, we were back at the conference table. Bonnie asked Leech and Grayson what it would take "to make this go away."

"Go away?" Alan Grayson said, chuckling softly. "Ms. Barker, *you're* the one who invited us here to discuss this case."

"We need to do more research," she said, holding her hands up like twin stop signs.

"Are you saying," Lawrence Leech asked, smiling, "that you're not prepared to adequately represent your clients? I know people who would have you *disbarred* for that."

"My client is not in a position at this time to make a settlement offer to you," Bonnie said. "He's a handyman, for God's sake."

Dad slung his arm around Bonnie's shoulder. "I'm

paying Bonnie here by building a deck on her house," he said, shrugging.

Oh God, Dad. This is not the time to get all chicken-fried and folksy.

I moved my chair slightly so that I could see more of the pool area. I watched Ben and Laura fight over a pair of swim goggles. Or maybe it was fins. With their voices muted by the thermal-glass window, it was hard to tell what they were fighting about. Someone — *Ben?* — threw the goggles in the pool. Now Laura was running around the pool, laughing. Or maybe she was crying. There went Sally, holding a fin in both hands over her head. It was like watching an aquarium.

"I don't think," said Alan Grayson, "that building a *deck* is an equitable satisfaction of the damages your son Charles has inflicted on Bargain Bonanza with his magazine essay."

"We have expert witnesses who can draw a straight line from his libelous words to our May, June, and July sales numbers," added Lawrence Leech. "And if our early back-to-school sales are any indication —"

That's when Ben and Laura tumbled into the Seagulls in Flight banquet room. They were both barefoot and dripping wet.

"Mom!" Laura yelled. "It's *my* turn for the flippers, and Ben won't let me have them."

"Be*cause*," Ben hollered over her, "Laura had the flippers *and* the goggles for *thirty* minutes! Clara timed her on her watch."

I could hear the unmistakable *clapclapclapclapclap* of Clara's flip-flops coming down the hallway. Sally was right behind her.

"Excuse us," Clara said, stepping into the banquet room. She adjusted the straps on her canary-yellow two-piece swimming suit.

"These are our other children," Mom said. "Kids, say hello to the lawyers from Bargain Bonanza."

"*Bargain Bonanza?*" said Ben. "Man, I'd give anything for a bag of Cowboy Cal Krusty Korn Chips right now."

"Me too," said Laura, forgetting to disagree with Ben. "Or a Cowboy Cal Kooky Cookie. The ones with the squiggly stripes of chocolate on top. Those are *sooooooooo* good."

"Mommy," said Sally. "Can I have a Cowboy Cal Kooky Cookie? *Pleeeeease?*"

I began sliding under the table. But as I did, I saw Alan Grayson lock eyes with Lawrence Leech. It was only for a split second, but I swear I saw something pass between them that was shark-like. It was predatory.

And right then, the colorful child's top that was our life began spinning slowly, wobbly, almost (haw) innocently.

7.

It's impossible to know if Sally's request for a Cowboy Cal Kooky Cookie was the reason. It could've been the freckles on Ben's nose. Or the sight of Clara's tan body, slick with water, in her yellow bathing suit.

For all I know, it might've been the master plan from the very beginning.

Whatever the reason, Leech and Grayson suggested we break for an early dinner — their treat — and then continue talking.

"I've got to leave to meet with another client," Bonnie said. She turned to Mom and Dad: "It's up to you guys."

"Let's keep talking," said Dad.

"We want to work this out," Mom added.

"Do what you want," Bonnie said, flipping her hair off her shoulder.

On her way out, she shook hands with Grayson and Leech and noted: "The food here is pretty good."

Mom walked Sally, Laura, Ben, and Clara back to the pool, where she helped them order sandwiches from a room-service menu. We did the same in the banquet room.

When Mom returned, Alan Grayson began speaking in a soft voice.

"We want to help you find a way out of this nightmare," he said, looking first to Mom and then to Dad. "We know how difficult this must be for you. Here you are, trying to raise a big family on a modest income. Well, not even *modest,* would you say?"

"We do all right," Dad said, looking down at his hands in a *just-us-dumb-old-Harrisongs* way.

"You're a carpenter?" Grayson continued. "Is that the correct word for what you do?"

"Frank can do anything," Mom said flatly. "He can build anything new. Fix anything old."

Alan Grayson smiled.

"You're lucky, Mrs. Harrison," he said. "My wife would be jealous. I am not what you'd call *handy.*"

Mom cleared her throat. "It's Harri*song.*"

"Of course," said Grayson.

"We obviously don't make the kind of money you

do," Mom continued. "But we make an honest living, for God's sake."

"Now *that's* an interesting statement," Lawrence Leech said. "An honest living. You work for a general contractor much of the time, Mr. Harri*song*. Is that right?"

"Yeah," Dad said.

"And I'm assuming you get a paycheck. Every two weeks?"

"That's right," said Dad.

"And your employer," pressed Leech, "the general contractor. He withholds state and federal taxes. Is that correct?"

"I feel like I'm on trial here," Dad said, laughing. "We probably shouldn't talk about these things without a lawyer."

"It's okay," Mom said. "We don't have anything to hide."

"Really?" prodded Leech. He was leaning his meaty white face across the table. "These other jobs you do on the side — the closets, the decks, the odd jobs. How are you paid for that work, Mr. Harrisong?"

"I . . . they . . . well, usually people just give me —" Dad began.

"Cash," Grayson said, as if enjoying the taste of the word. "Just like the jobs you did back in Normal. It was always cash, wasn't it? Has it ever occurred to you that you should report that income to the Internal Revenue Service?"

"It's not that much," Dad said. "Not more than . . . I'm not even sure, really."

"You're not *sure?*" Leech said. He stood up and began walking around the table.

"You don't keep track of your income?" Grayson asked. "Then how do you know how much you owe in taxes? Much easier simply not to file, isn't it?"

Dad was looking out the window. His eyes were glassy.

"What is this?" Mom asked. *"What?"*

I could feel the air in the room changing. It was getting closer, tighter, like the air before a tornado, when animals start doing weird things.

"I got . . . I got a little behind on all that stuff," Dad said. "Back in Normal, there was so much paperwork. I didn't have a bookkeeper."

A bead of sweat rolled down his face.

"I mean," Dad continued, trying to smile. "I was doing the best I could. Some years it was food and clothes for the kids — or paying taxes."

"Tax evasion," said Alan Grayson, "is a federal crime."

"I . . . I just . . . I," Dad sputtered. He was laughing nervously.

Mom stared at him. Her face was a giant question mark.

"We need to take a break," she said, echoing Bonnie.

"No breaks," Grayson stated, almost spitting the words. "We have a seven o'clock flight that we intend to make."

I looked at the clock on the wall: 5:05.

Our dinner arrived on a squeaky cart, wheeled in by a pimply teenager. I ate half a club sandwich and a handful of French fries while Mom and Dad signed their names — fifty, maybe one hundred times — to a stack of papers. Lawrence Leech made sure they signed each page.

"You realize," Grayson said, "that Bargain Bonanza has never done anything like this before. You'll be the first."

Silence. Mom and Dad didn't even look up from the papers.

Now Mom was starting to cry. Oh God. She was holding a hand up to her face. Alan Grayson reached across the table and touched her hand. I thought Mom would swat him away, but she didn't.

"Hey," Grayson said softly. "This isn't so bad. Believe me."

No response from Mom. *Good.*

Lawrence Leech was stacking the papers loudly.

"So you'll need to get your things packed up," he said. "I don't know how much you have or where it —"

Mom fell apart.

"Will we be able to see the children?" she said, choking

on her tears. "When we're in prison. The children. Can they visit?"

Lawrence Leech and Alan Grayson looked at each other.

"*Prison?*" said Leech. "No one's going to prison."

"You're going to Dallas," said Grayson. "Your whole family's going."

"Perhaps we haven't made this clear," Leech said. "You've just agreed to be Bargain Bonanza's first spokesfamily."

"Spokes*what?*" Dad asked.

"Spokes*family*," repeated Leech. "You and your family will represent Bargain Bonanza at trade shows and conventions. You'll do some commercial work. Help launch new product lines."

"We'll be paid for this?" Mom asked.

"That'll be determined on a project-by-project basis," Leech said. "The real value of this arrangement is that you'll have no expenses. You'll live at El Rancho. That's the office-shopping-condo complex owned by Bargain Bonanza. And you'll get ten thousand dollars a month in Bargain Bonanza Buckeroos that you can use for groceries, clothing, toiletries — anything you want at Bargain Bonanza, Bargain BIG-Bonanza, Bargain Bonanza Extravaganza, and Bargain Bonanza SuperFantastic Stores."

Lawrence Leech looked at his watch. "We needed to

leave ten minutes ago," he said. He reached across the table to shake Dad's hand and then Mom's. He looked at me for the first time all day.

"Have you ever been to Dallas, young man?" he asked.

"No," I said.

"You'll like it, especially El Rancho," he said. "It's Bargain Bonanza's most elegant property."

Alan Grayson was giving Dad an envelope and instructions: "Just pack for a day or two. The movers will probably beat you there."

The lawyers left. Mom, Dad, and I remained in the banquet room. The greasy smell of our unfinished dinners hung like a dense fog around us.

"We're not going to tell the little kids about the taxes," Mom said softly.

Little kids was how Mom and Dad still referred to Ben, Laura, and Sally.

"Or Clara," said Dad. He looked at me. "Okay, Charles?"

"Okay," I said. "I won't tell."

We walked in silence to the pool area.

"Just ten minutes more?" Laura cried when she saw us. *"Pleeeease?"*

"It's time to go," said Dad. His voice was old and tired.

"Not yet," said Mom, sitting sidesaddle on a plastic

chair. Her eyes followed a yellow cab as it pulled away from the motel. "I don't want them to know we're walking home."

*   *   *

We spent that August night packing. We still had the seven suitcases we'd brought with us from Normal.

Sally wailed about having to miss the first day of school.

"I've only been practicing my *Rs all* summer," she pouted.

Ben wasn't thrilled about leaving, either. "Just as long as we're back by Halloween," he said, stuffing a pile of wadded clothes into his suitcase. "Dylan says the candy they give out in his neighborhood is awesome."

"It's so unfair how we *always* have to leave our friends," Laura cried. "Our *best* friends."

It boggled my brain that Laura had *best* friends. I'd never had any real friends except Clara — and she didn't count because she was my sister.

To punish myself for uprooting my family (again), I packed my collection of haunted house mysteries in a box and left it behind the trailer.

The next morning, a black limousine picked us up at seven o'clock. We all piled in the spacious backseat except for Dad, who sat in the front, next to the driver.

"What about the *O'Migosh*?" I asked on the ride to the airport.

"We're paid at the dock through next July," Dad said, without turning around. "We'll be back by then."

The thought of leaving our houseboat made my stomach hurt. Decrepit and unreliable as it was, the *O'Migosh* was our home. For almost three years, we'd never been more than a short walk from it. Now we were leaving the *O'Migosh* to fend for itself. I patted the front pocket of my jeans where I kept my key to the houseboat on the seashell keychain. The $1,200 was in my billfold in my back pocket.

"I almost forgot we used to live on a houseboat," Sally said as we glided down the highway. "That was fun."

"It wasn't *that* fun," Ben muttered. "We never got to see any sharks or pirates. We didn't even get stranded on a desert island. We never get to do anything fun."

"We'll save the pirates for the next time," Dad promised. "You've always gotta save something for the next adventure."

I remembered Lawrence Leech circling the conference table in the Seagulls in Flight banquet room and Alan Grayson accusing us of being pirates.

This, I thought, *was our next adventure.*

8.

I now understand enough about moviemaking to know that this is the part of the story where the tempo changes. If the producers of *Normal* had made this movie instead — the classic story-behind-the-story — they would play an upbeat pop song right now. The director would do this next bit as a series of quick cuts, like a music video.

Open with us on the flight to Dallas. Freeze-frame on my family sitting in first class. Add sound effect of an old-timey camera shutter. *CLICK WHIR.*

Footage of us in the airport limo. Freeze-frame on Ben and Laura pawing through the tiny minibar while Clara looks out the window at the Dallas skyline. *CLICK WHIR.*

Footage of us arriving at El Rancho, a mirrored colossus of shops (ground floor, mezzanine), offices (floors 2 through 78), and condos (floors 79 through 92). Tight shot on the desk clerk instructing the bellhop to carry our luggage. Make sure the actor who plays the bellhop flinches visibly when his gloved hand makes contact with our comically mildewed suitcases. Freeze-frame on Dad turning the key to our ninety-second-floor condo. *CLICK WHIR.*

Footage of us wandering through the condo. Close-up of the marble floors. The front hall with the huge, fake-flower arrangement on the dainty glass table. The sleek silver-and-black kitchen. The circular living / dining room with the curved floor-to-ceiling windows overlooking downtown Dallas.

Cut to a shot of Laura, saucer-eyed, realizing there are enough bedrooms for all of us kids to have his/her own room. Cut to Ben sliding in his socks down the front hallway. Freeze-frame on Sally jumping on her bed and Clara laughing. Maybe add a shot of me staring up at *The Collector's Editions of Charles Dickens* on the top shelf of the living room bookcase. *CLICK WHIR.*

Cut to the concierge teaching us how to open and lock the front door to the condo from the inside. Footage of each of us tapping the security code into the doorside panel. Follow with concierge teaching us how to call a Bargain Bonanza limo by simply dialing *7 on any of the phones.

Maybe use a digital effect to take the roof off El Rancho so you can see how our condo is shaped like an octopus: the round living/dining room head in the center, and eight ten-tacle-like rooms — six bedrooms, most with private baths, one kitchen, one laundry room.

Cut to us unpacking. Freeze-frame on Mom opening her closet and finding a new wardrobe. She holds her hands over her heart. Freeze-frame on all of us opening the closets in our bedrooms and finding new wardrobes. Zoom in on the tags on the clothes. Freeze-frame on the words: *Bargain Bonanza.* Fade out music as we slowly dissolve to: THE NEXT MORNING.

* * *

Dad almost burned El Rancho down the next morning when he tried to make toast in the oven broiler.

"No worries," said the concierge, who arrived to turn off the fire alarms. He also gave us brief how-to lessons on all the high-tech stuff in the condo, including the home theater in the living room, the ice maker in the fridge, and the ultra-modern showers none of us could figure out. And, of course, the toaster.

Mom refused to let Ben wear a cowboy hat to our ten o'clock meeting with the Brand Identity division of Bargain Bonanza.

"But it was in my closet," Ben said. "So that means they *want* me to wear it."

It was a question we had all asked that morning: *Were we supposed to wear the Bargain Bonanza clothes hanging in our closet to the meeting?* Mom had ruled yes because the condo clothes were cleaner than anything we'd brought with us from the trailer.

I'd forgotten how much I despised the scratchy feel of those cheap Bargain Bonanza clothes against my skin. Or how much I hated to see my dad dressed in an outfit from Bargain Bonanza's Dude Dad line. It all brought back a million bad memories of Normal.

"Gentlemen don't wear hats inside," Mom told Ben as we walked through the underground tunnel that connected El Rancho to Bargain Bonanza's corporate offices.

"Pirates do," Ben insisted. "Kings do — if you consider a crown a hat."

"Men who make doughnuts wear hats inside," Laura added helpfully.

"Santa wears a hat in his workshop," Sally said.

She began singing "Jingle Bells" in the echo chamber-like tunnel. Laura joined in.

"Shhhhhh!" Mom said. "Settle down *now*. You're acting like a bunch of savages. I want church manners from everyone."

"Church manners?" Ben yelped. "Are we going to have to start going to *church* again?"

"Maybe," said Mom.

We hadn't been to Mass more than three or four times since we left Normal. I knew that bothered Mom. Earlier that morning I'd heard her asking the concierge for directions to the Cathedral Santuario de Guadalupe in downtown Dallas. To her delight, it was in walking distance of El Rancho.

"This is an important meeting we're going to," Mom lectured as we paraded through the tunnel. "I want everyone to pay attention. I'm going to be asking you questions about it later."

"Are we homeschooling again?" Laura whined.

"Yes," Mom said. She looked to Dad for support.

"This will be a good business class for you all," he said. "Pretend this is your first day of school."

Brand Identity — or B.I., as it was called — was on the twenty-second floor. Corporate slogans filled the walls: *Bargain Bonanza: Making BIG Dreams Come True for the LITTLE Guy. Bargain Bonanza: So Many Things for So Many People. Saving YOU Money Makes US Smile.*

The receptionist clapped her hands when we got off the

elevator. "The Harrisong family!" she cheered. "Welcome aboard!"

She led us to a room where nine people — seven men, two women — were seated around a long, glossy conference table. Everyone stood up when we entered.

"Here they are!" It was Lawrence Leech.

"Any trouble with the flight?" he asked, putting his arm around Dad's shoulder. "Everything okay in the condo? Glad to hear they put you in the penthouse. The view is something else, isn't it? Hi there, princess." He patted Sally on the head. Then he made the introductions.

There was Richard, who was the Brand Identity division chief. Jerry, who did all the B.I. licensing. Linda, who was in charge of focus groups. Mark, who oversaw U.S. and Canadian marketing. (*Mark in marketing. Finally, one I could remember.*) Iris was involved in Asia. Kurt handled trade shows and conventions. Carlos did something with Latin America. A cool-looking guy named Brandon with thick black hair tied in a ponytail handled dramatic rights.

"And you already know me," Lawrence Leech said. "I just do the boring legal work. These are the people who make things happen. They'll take good care of you. Kids, if the meeting gets boring, you can feed the birds."

He pointed to a row of metal cages next to the windows. They were filled with gaudy, exotic birds. A parrot glared at us and squawked.

After Mr. Leech left, Richard took over. He was thirty-something years old and had thin, blond hair combed straight back from his forehead. I found out later he swam every morning before work, which explained his chlorine-y smell and bloodshot eyes.

"What can we get you?" Richard asked. "Coffee? Tea? Soda? Kids, how 'bout a Bargain Bonanza Cowboy Cal Cola?"

"Sure!" Ben said.

A flurry of activity followed as cold cans of Cowboy Cal Cola and frosted glasses were placed in front of us.

"This is *so* cool," Laura said. "We *never* get a whole can to ourself."

Polite laughter all around.

"So," Richard said. "I guess I should begin by saying how excited we all are to acquire this property."

Mom and Dad exchanged a nervous look.

"I think there's been a mistake," said Dad. "We don't have any property — except a houseboat, and I don't think you'd find it very exciting."

"Sorry," Richard said, smiling. "I hate shoptalk and I'm the worst offender. What I meant by *property* is the story of your family. We're really excited to start developing product lines based on your family."

"And your experiences on the S.S. *O'Migosh*," Linda chimed in. "There are so many fun things we can do with that."

"Speaking of the famous *O'Migosh,* where is it now?" asked Brandon.

"Alabama," Dad answered. "In dry dock. I was doing some repairs on it."

"I guess we could have it moved to the lot," Richard said to Brandon.

"No, no," Brandon said, dismissing the idea with his hand. "We'll just get photos of it. That's all we need. Frank, you can get me the address of the dry dock, right? I'll send someone over there to take photos."

"Photos?" Mom asked. "Of our houseboat?"

"We need pictures so we can build a replica," Brandon said. "For the movie."

"*Movie?!*" asked Laura, beaming.

"I thought Leech and Grayson explained all this to you," said Brandon. "Bargain Bonanza's producing a movie about your family based on Charles's magazine article. We're calling it *Normal.*"

"We're going to be in a *movie!*" Ben cried. His mouth hung open like a happy dog.

"Not *you,* exactly," Brandon said carefully. "Actors *playing* you. Don't worry. We'll audition hundreds of boys till we find the right actor to play you."

"*I* could be me," Ben said with dignity.

More laughter all around.

"Acting is boring," Richard explained. "We're saving you to do the fun stuff."

The B.I. team showed us the Short-Term Marketing Plan (STMP) and Long-Range Marketing Plan (LRMP). Both had a calendar with target dates circled. Launch of NormalWear line of clothing. Soft goods. Footwear. Film.

I turned to look at Clara. She looked back at me and crossed her eyes.

"As you can see," said Richard, "we don't have a lot of time. It's almost September, and the first run of clothes has to be in stores by January. The film is booked for release in April."

"The good thing," said Linda excitedly, "is that we've already focus-grouped you."

A woman popped her head in the door. "I thought the

meeting was at ten thirty," she said. She held a motorcycle helmet against her hip.

"We changed it to ten," Brandon said.

"Is this them?" the woman asked, pointing to us as she sidled in the room and sat on the window ledge.

"Yes," said Richard. "These are the Harrisongs. And this is Sophie Buchanan. She heads up our publicity department."

If Mom had a younger, cooler sister, she would've looked like Sophie Buchanan. Sophie's hair was curly like Mom's. But, unlike Mom, Sophie didn't try to control it. She wore it long and messy. The first time I saw her, I thought she'd forgotten to brush it. Later, I realized this was Sophie's style.

At that first meeting, she wore what I discovered was her uniform: black jeans and a boy's white T-shirt with a man's suit jacket over it. (None of it from Bargain Bonanza, of course.) A book bag-like satchel was slung diagonally across her chest.

Sophie stared at each of us individually and then as a group.

"I gotta say," she said, biting her bottom lip, "I don't know whose idea it was to get you, but it's the smartest damn thing this place has done in a long time. Using real people who actually shop at Bargain Bonanza. It's inspired. Much better than the talking pony campaign. Though that was certainly cute, Brandon. Cute, cute, cute."

"Okay, Sophie," Brandon snapped. "We're trying to work here. Do you mind? We were talking about the focus group results."

"Focus groups," repeated Mom. She was taking notes on a paper napkin.

"That's right," Richard said. "We brought in ordinary shoppers and presented you to them."

He pushed a thick report titled *Meet the Harrisongs!* toward the middle of the table. Mom opened it. The first page was an enlarged photo of our family. I recognized it immediately as one of our old photo Christmas cards.

"Where in the world did you get this?" Mom asked, thumbing through the report. It contained all of our Christmas cards and school photos — even Mom's and Dad's senior pictures from high school.

"Oh, that's the easy part," said Linda.

"The challenge," said Richard, "is figuring out what products you'd be best suited for." He was standing in front of a wipe board now.

"Sally," Richard continued, writing her name and an equals sign, "will do print and broadcast spots for Bargain

Bonanza toys, learning materials, in-house baked goods, and licensed cookies and candies."

Sally sucked on the ends of her hair as she watched Richard write *Toys* and *Sweets* next to her name.

"Laura and Clara," Richard said as he printed their names, "will model Bargain Bonanza clothing."

"Yes!" Laura said, pumping her hand in the air. Mom pulled it down.

"As for Ben . . ." Richard said slowly. "He's an interesting one."

"Tell us about it," said Dad wearily.

"The focus group really responded to Ben," Richard said. "But they wondered if he might be . . . maybe a little autistic?"

"Ben's not artistic!" Laura said, chortling. "Clara's artistic, but not Ben. I'm ten times more artistic than Ben."

"Ben is *not* autistic," Mom said stiffly. "Not in the least."

"It's just that his face is so expressive, you know?" Linda said. "He'd work really well in Bargain Bonanza's Handi-Capable line of products."

Ben shrugged modestly. "I'm not really very handy," he said. "Now Dad's handy."

Dad took over. "I'm not sure where you're going with

this, but Ben here is a really bright guy. And for you or the focus group to imply that —"

"Okay, okay," said Richard. "I was just throwing that out there for discussion. Because if he *was,* you know, we could use that. Um . . . what else did we have for Ben?"

Linda riffled through her papers.

"Electronics," she said. "Footwear. Watches."

"Oh, you'll like this," said Richard, with the strained smile of a preschool teacher. "We're developing a wristwatch based on Ben. We're calling it the Little Benny."

"Benny?" Ben said, slumping over in his chair.

"You've heard of Big Ben in London?" Mark in Marketing asked. "The big clock? Well, you'd be Little Benny. We'd shoot the commercials on-site. You'd get to go to London."

"Hey," Mom said, elbowing Ben. "That'd be fun."

"I guess," Ben said dejectedly. Even he wasn't buying Mom's fake enthusiasm.

"These watches are going to be really cool," Richard said. "Waterproof, fireproof, three time zones."

No reaction from Ben.

"You know what?" Richard said. "I can see a picture of your face on the watch."

"Really?" said Ben, a sly smile creeping across his face. "That'd be okay, I guess."

I saw Sophie wink at Ben. She was feeding a parrot a tiny piece of her bagel. She was pretty.

Mom and Dad were "no-brainers," according to Richard. Bargain Bonanza's design team would develop a new line of tools that Dad would promote.

"For the Normal guy who does odd jobs," Brandon said. "For the man who can fix anything."

I recognized the line from my magazine article. Ponytailed Brandon was filching my lines.

They also saw Dad and Ben "showcasing" a line of camping and fishing equipment. Mom would be the *spokesmother* for Bargain Bonanza–brand soft goods (towels, sheets, pillowcases, pot holders), housewares, and boxed dinners.

"What about Charles?" Laura asked.

I was hoping they'd forgotten me.

"Charles was something of a mystery to the focus group," Richard said, looking at his bound copy of *Results from the Harrisong Family Focus Group Assessment.*

"The participants suggested a name change," Richard said, reading from the text. "They discussed possible new names: Charlie, Carl, Chad, Thad, and Chuck . . . before arriving at the name and character they liked best: *Chaz*."

"*Chaz?*" I said.

"Very contemporary," said Linda.

"Edgy," Richard agreed. "They weren't sure what product lines you'd be best for. Their only suggestion was that we use you for our OTC line."

"*OTC?*" I asked.

"Over-the-counter medicine," Linda said. "Things you don't need a prescription for, like allergy pills and vitamins."

"Vitamins would be good," said Richard. "Because they found you a little . . . well, not as energetic as the others. Not as, you know, *active*."

"Oh," said Linda, looking through her papers. "And laxatives, too. Charles would be perfect to promote the new line of Cowboy Chaz laxatives."

9.

Of course I refused. Downright, flat-out refused.

"I am *not* doing a commercial for *laxatives,*" I told Mom and Dad on Sunday night. "I would rather *die.*"

It was after dinner. Clara was in her room, painting. Sally was in the living room, watching a nature show on TV. Ben and Laura were sock-sliding up and down the marble front hallway. Mom, Dad, and I were in the kitchen.

"One thing at a time," Mom said, turning to Dad. "How long will you and Ben be gone?"

"We're supposed to be in the lobby tomorrow morning at nine," said Dad. "They said it'll take all day. We're doing a photo shoot at a state park called Enchanted Rock something-or-other."

"And Charles," Mom said, "you're supposed to be in the lobby tomorrow at eight thirty. For your . . . thing?"

"I'm *not* doing it," I said. "I'm not. Mom, do I *have* to do it?"

Mom looked at Dad, who stood up and walked into the living room.

"At least you'll get to ride in a limousine to the Bargain Bonanza film lot," Mom offered tentatively as she began unloading the dishwasher.

"I don't care about *that*," I said. "Who cares about a stupid *limousine?* I'm not Ben."

"Clara doesn't want to do her photo shoot tomorrow, either," Mom admitted. She was transferring silverware from the dishwasher to a drawer. "I'm not sure how much say we have in all of this. Frank?"

No answer from the living room.

"Dad?"

Silence.

Mom began stacking clean dinner plates loudly in a cupboard. I went to my room.

I spent that night trying to negotiate with God:

Dear God, I'll do anything but this. If You make me do a laxative commercial, I'll look like an idiot. And I'm not an idiot. (Am I?) Come on, God. Get me out of this, okay? Please? Thank You. Amen.

"I'm not doing this," I told Mark in Marketing when I arrived at the Bargain Bonanza film lot the next morning. We were standing in front of a canoe that had a white porcelain toilet in the center.

"Just have fun with it," Mark said, slapping me on the back. "Brandon's a great director. He'll take good care of you."

A woman named Justine handed me clothes and pushed me into a dressing room. I pulled on a pair of blue shorts and a green shirt the color of seasickness. Both were way too big for me.

"Park it right here!" Crystal, the makeup artist, ordered playfully when I came out of the dressing room.

I sat on a stool in front of a mirror while Crystal dusted my face and eyelashes with white powder. Then, using the tip of her middle finger, she gently dabbed purple cream under my eyes.

"You're supposed to look constipated," Crystal explained. "Here, drink this."

She handed me a glass filled with orange fizzy liquid. "A vitamin cocktail," she said.

Crystal pulled a hair dryer out of a drawer and began blowing the hair in front of my face while I drank the tangy beverage. She parted my hair in the center and slicked it down. My eyes met hers in the mirror.

"I look awful," I said.

"That's the idea," she said. "You're gonna be a pro, kid."

"Okay, let's GO!" Brandon was yelling. "Where's the water?"

Giant screens descended from the ceiling, filling the area behind the canoe.

"Where's the video?" Brandon hollered.

On his cue, digital images of water and sky appeared on the screens.

"Good," yelled Brandon. "Now where's Charlie?"

I hid behind a monitor. I could see only the back of Brandon's ponytail.

"Charlie!" Brandon said, spying me. "Come on. Let's see how this commode fits you. You've got your lines, right? No? It's real easy. You can read from the monitor, if you want. Or just memorize the script. If I were you —"

"I'm . . . I'm . . . I'm not —" I stammered. "I'm not going to sit on a toi —"

"Don't worry," Brandon said. "I'm shooting you from the waist up. And, look, it's not a real toilet. There's no plumbing. It's just a chair in a boat. Script! I need a script."

A girl with a clipboard rushed over. She handed the script to Brandon. He passed it to me to read.

```
            GOTTA GO (:20 SPOT)

COWBOY CHAZ sits with pained expression on a
toilet plopped comically in the center of
a canoe.

VOICE-OVER: Maintaining regularity can be a
challenge, even for Normal people.

COWBOY CHAZ: That's why I rely on Cowboy
Chaz's Gotta Go. Because when you've Gotta Go,
you've gotta go.

(SOUND OF FLUSH as CANOE is shown descending
waterfall.)

VOICE-OVER: Aaaaaaiiiiiiiiiiiiiii!

(SPLASH!)
```

"That middle stuff is yours," said Brandon, looking through a viewfinder on one of the cameras. "The 'That's-why-I-rely-on' bit. I know it seems sorta crude, but trust me on this. With commercials, you want simple. The simpler the better."

"I . . . I really just don't like this," I mumbled. "Not at all."

Brandon looked at me hard.

"You know what I don't like?" he asked quietly, crouching down to speak directly in my ear. "Your attitude. This is your job now. So let's stop fussing like a little old lady and get to work. Okay, Charlie?"

I stared at my new tennis shoes. I wondered how the people at Bargain Bonanza knew what size shoes I wore.

"*Okay?*" Brandon said.

"Why can't I do something —" I started.

"What?" Brandon barked. "What do you want to do?"

"Something that has to do with, you know, like, writing," I said. "Maybe I could write some books, mysteries maybe, that Bargain Bonanza could sell in bins. In the back of the store?"

"Nobody wants to read your crap," Brandon said. He sighed loudly. Then he rubbed his eyes. "Look," he said with a reluctant gentleness. "You didn't get this gig because you're a *writer*. They chose you for this because you're so *normal*. You could be anyone. Charlie, look at me."

I raised my eyes slightly. I hadn't noticed his gold stud earring before.

"I can make you a star," Brandon whispered. "Just do what I tell you."

I walked down a plywood plank, remembering how much I hated adventures, and climbed in the canoe. As I sat on the toilet, Crystal repowdered my nose. After fifteen minutes of test shots, Brandon said I didn't look "cowboy" enough, so Justine found a leather vest for me to wear over the green shirt.

Forty-five minutes later, Brandon approved the lighting. When he finally gave the order to roll film, I felt a wave of nausea roll over me, followed by a spasm in my gut.

"I'm sorry, but I've really got to go," I said, stumbling out of the canoe. "I have to use the restroom."

Only I would get diarrhea filming a laxative commercial.

An hour later, we were on take 23. Brandon pointed at me, and I read the text scrolling down the TelePrompTer:

"That's why I . . . um . . . . rely on Cowboy . . . . uh, Chaz's . . . Got To Go —"

"CUT!" Brandon screamed. "*Gotta.* Not *Got To. Gotta.* Just relax, would you?"

"I've got to go again," I said, climbing out of the canoe.

I ran to the men's room. This time, I barely made it in time to drop my shorts before the brown liquid began filling the toilet. I could hear the laughter in the studio. Then I heard the bathroom door open.

"Charles?"

It was a woman's voice.

"Charles?" the voice repeated. "It's me, Sophie Buchanan."

"This is the *men's* room," I said.

"I know. Can I come in?"

"Why?"

My eyes dropped. I could see her boots — black, square-toed biker boots.

"Charles, I wanted to tell you something."

"Can you wait till I'm done?"

I heard the sound of her body sliding down the wall. She was sitting on the floor, next to the sink. I straightened my back.

Could she see me? How bad did it smell in here? God!

"I just wanted to say you're doing a really good job, Charles."

"Yeah, right."

"Okay," she conceded. "You're doing a really lousy job. The worst ever."

It almost made me laugh. I didn't dare, lest I lose control of my bowels.

"I'm terrible at this stuff," I said.

"I know," she said. "You're a disaster. But I'll tell you something. You have more class in your little finger than that whole roomful of people out there."

"Unh," I mumbled.

"I mean it," she said. "Being a phony doesn't come easy to you. You'd be surprised how natural it is for a lot of people to just spew this crap."

An odd thing to say to a person who one minute earlier had literally been spewing crap. The same thought must've occurred to her.

"What I mean," she said, "is that you're not a very good liar. That makes you worthless to people like Richard and Brandon who need other people to tell their lies."

The smell was closing in on me.

"I have to flush," I said, pushing down the silver lever. The sound of water refilling the toilet was momentarily comforting. "Sorry, but I . . . I'm not done yet."

I was trying to give her the cue to leave.

"That's fine," she said.

I could see her shifting her weight on the floor. *Why wouldn't she leave?*

"I wonder if it's something you ate?" she asked.

I remembered the vitamin cocktail Crystal had given me. I told Sophie about it.

"Probably just sodium pills ground up in fruit juice," she said. "She was trying to make you retain water so you'd look puffy and, you know, constipated."

My bowels chose that moment to let loose.

"Obviously, it didn't work," she said. "Why don't you flush again?"

I did. I felt so light-headed.

"You don't have to stay in here," I said. "It smells gross."

"It's okay," she said. "I've changed poopy diapers worse than this. I have a son."

She didn't look like a mother.

"How old is he?" I asked.

"Fourteen," she said.

We sat in silence.

"Why do you work here?" I finally asked.

"What?"

"If you hate Richard and Brandon so much, why do you work here?"

"I don't *hate* them," she clarified. "Maybe I don't totally respect them. And I don't, because Richard's an idiot and Brandon's a pig. But . . . I don't know. The money's good. I've got a kid, like I said. Plus, you know what?"

"What?"

"You're not going to believe me, but I like Bargain Bonanza. Or at least I believe in the idea behind it. I think there oughta be places for people to buy cheap stuff, like laxatives. Charles, think about it. There are people in this world who are not blessed with bowels as — shall we say — *athletic* as yours. So why not help them save a buck on laxatives? I believe in helping the little guy. And I pray to God I never have to shop there myself." She took a breath. "Feel any better?"

"I'm not sure. Maybe."

"Come on," she said. "We better get back out there."

The funny thing was, I did feel a little better. I flushed and zipped. Sophie was standing in front of the sink when I came out of the stall. I washed my hands and looked at her in the mirror.

"Who started this place?" I asked.

"The Bargain Bonanza film lot?" she said. She was looking at herself in the mirror and finger-combing her hair.

"No," I said. "The whole place. Bargain Bonanza."

"The founder?" she said, wiping a smudge of lipstick from her teeth. "I'm not sure what his name is. I know he's a billionaire. He doesn't have much to do with the place now. He started it, but then basically turned everything over to the morons in middle management. He lives in Geneva."

She looked at me in the mirror. "There's no Cowboy Cal, if that's what you thought," she said with mock sincerity. "I hope I'm not disillusioning you."

"You're not," I said. "It's what I always sort of imagined."

We were standing at the door.

"Take a deep breath before you go back out there," she said. "You can do this."

I breathed in deeply. "It stinks in here," I said.

She laughed. Sophie had a low, scratchy laugh that appealed to me immediately.

"Be quiet and breathe," she said. "Exhale. Now do it again. Inhale and hold it. Now exhale."

I did what she said. It felt good to breathe.

"What's your son's name?" I said on the second exhale.

"James. Keep breathing."

I took a breath. Held it. Exhaled.

"James Buchanan?" I asked. "Like the president?"

"Of course," she said. "How could I resist?"

Somehow I knew without asking there wasn't a husband in the picture. That's when she pushed up her left sleeve and showed me her tattoo.

" 'Believe,' " I said, reading the purplish-black word on her arm. "Believe in *what?*"

"I don't care," she said. "A kid. God. Bargain Bonanza. Anything. Just pick something and believe in it."

"Is that your philosophy?"

"My *philosophy?*" she said. "You must be a Leo. When's your birthday?"

"July twenty-eighth," I said.

"I knew it. You're a Leo, like me."

"Is that bad?"

"No," she said. "Leos are cool. We're the lions. Creative, idealistic, philosophically inclined. Our ruling planet is the sun."

"How old are you?" I asked.

"Thirty-four," she said. "Okay, thirty-eight."

She smiled. It was a funny, crooked smile that made me smile, too.

I finally got my lines right — or at least to Brandon's satisfaction — on take 47. I visited the restroom one last time to change clothes and splash cold water on my face.

As I rode in the limo back to the condo, I held my stomach. It was flat and empty, but I wasn't hungry — not for food, anyway. I knew I needed something; some kind of nourishment to get me through this.

Back then I still didn't know what it was. All I knew was that God had refused to negotiate with me. Not only that, He'd thrown in diarrhea on top of it.

Then it hit me: God couldn't negotiate with me. He had to punish me for writing that stupid magazine article — and for my prideful prayer to be wonderful and unusual in some small (or big) way.

That was it. I was getting exactly what I deserved, which, interestingly enough, was exactly what I'd asked for.

God. Only You would think of something like this.

10.

It was November before Ben remembered we'd missed Halloween in Alabama. He'd spent the last week of October in London with a Bargain Bonanza crew, filming commercials for Little Benny watches. It was Ben's first trip away from home alone, other than sleepovers at Dylan Goodman's house.

At first, Mom and Dad opposed the trip — until Lawrence Leech resurfaced and showed them clause 79(a) subsection 3 of the contract, "wherein the Harrisong family agrees to travel together or individually, domestically or internationally, to research, launch, and/or promote new products and/or services offered by Bargain Bonanza or any of its licensees."

Ben was characteristically blasé about the whole thing.

"Who's going to remind me to put on deodorant?" he

asked Mom before he left. That was his only fear about traveling abroad.

Ben returned from London with the swagger of a world traveler and a Little Benny watch for each of us. Someone had engraved our names on the back.

"They don't have Halloween over there in England," Ben said on his first night back in the condo. He was digging through a bowl of fun-sized Bargain Bonanza Halloween candy Mom had picked up out of habit.

"Don't feel bad," said Laura, suddenly interested in the candy that had sat untouched on the kitchen counter for a week. "'Cause we didn't get to go trick-or-treating, either."

So we celebrated Halloween that night. It was Dad's idea for everyone — even him and Mom — to dress up. Mom pulled together a gypsy costume. Dad put on a flannel shirt and jeans and said he was a lumberjack.

Laura made cat ears out of black construction paper and asked Mom to draw whiskers on her face. Sally tried to follow suit until Laura objected.

"She can't be what *I* am!" Laura moaned.

"Go as a copycat, Sal," suggested Ben. He was simply waving his passport and pointing to his new Bargain Bonanza luggage, claiming he was an international pilot.

Mom turned Sally's cat whiskers into mouse whiskers. A piece of Cowboy Cal Head-a-Chedda' Cheese from the fridge served as her prop.

Clara and I said we were too old for costumes, but the others insisted we dress up.

"Okay, then, I'm the *Mona Lisa*," said Clara.

She found an empty picture frame in her stash of Bargain Bonanza art supplies and held it in front of her face.

"Charles, what are you?" Laura asked.

"I'm reading," I said.

On our most recent shopping trip to Bargain Bonanza, I'd picked up a dozen Cowboy Cal comic books. I justified them to Mom as a necessary balance to my college textbooks — and because I was too lazy to tackle *The Collector's Editions of Charles Dickens* in the living room that Mom said was part of my new homeschool curriculum.

"Come on," begged Laura. "You have to be *somebody*."

"Okay, I'm Mark in Marketing," I said.

Only Clara laughed.

Mom let each of us choose a bag of candy from the pantry. Then she sent us to our bedrooms. We took turns trick-or-treating to one another's rooms.

"Trick or treat, Mark in Marketing," Clara said when

she knocked on my door. She held the picture frame up to her face and smiled mysteriously.

"Hey, Mona," I said, dropping three Cowboy Cal Choco-rific Choco-bombs in her bag. "Or do you go by *Lisa* these days?"

"*Mona*'s fine," she said, returning two Choco-bombs to my bag. "I don't really like these things. Don't take it personally, Markety Mark."

"I won't. Actually, I'm not Mark in Marketing."

"Who are you?" she laughed. "Iris in Asia?"

"No," I said. "I guess I'm just . . . a little depressed."

"Really?" she asked. "I'm kinda enjoying this. It can't last forever."

My fear was that it just might. Then again, it depended on how long God intended to punish me.

After everyone was in bed, I went out to the living room and stared at the night sky. It was a deep, mottled blue. I looked down on the tiny streetlights and toylike cars. *I'm ninety-two floors above the ground,* I reminded myself.

But living on the houseboat had distorted my perception. I felt ninety-two floors above water, not earth. Like I was on an enormous ship moving slowly, inevitably toward something dark and dangerous.

I longed to feel grounded. I remembered my beloved collection of haunted house mysteries and how safe they always made me feel. Books could do that for me.

I decided to try tackling *The Collector's Editions of Charles Dickens* after all. I stood on the edge of the sofa and reached for *Great Expectations*. But when I tried to pull the glossy red volume from the bookshelf, I found it was connected to the rest of the books. They weren't books at all, but a hollow wooden decoration designed to look like a shelf full of books.

I returned to the window and looked for stars. I needed a little piece of reality right then, but I couldn't find any stars. The lights from El Rancho drowned them out.

* * *

The launch of NormalWear was historic on two fronts, Richard told us at our next Wednesday morning meeting with the Brand Identity division.

"This is the first time anyone has ever launched an exclusive line of clothing and lifestyle products based on an actual American family," Richard gushed. "And we've got almost *seven* entire lines ready to roll."

The official launch of NormalWear was slated to take place in January at the What's Next? show in Las Vegas.

"It's where manufacturers and retailers show off all the

new fashions and products," Iris said. "It's always *super* exciting."

"We'll have you at Bargain Bonanza's booth most of the time," Mark explained. "I'm sure Sophie will have some publicity events she'll want you to do. Right, Sophie?"

"Yep," Sophie said, not looking up from her legal pad. She was drawing loopy flowers.

"And you'll let us know what those are?" asked Brandon, glaring at Sophie.

"Aye-aye, Captain," she said, now gazing out the window.

I loved Sophie's sarcasm. I also loved how she never looked at people she didn't like.

"There's still a ton of work to be done before the launch," Richard said, distributing our schedules for the next six weeks.

Dad spent countless hours with Bargain Bonanza's industrial design team, deciding which tools to include in the Frankly Tools line. Mom was working on a line of crafts and sewing kits. She did her own narration for these spots: "Crafts for women with enough on their plates already!"

Sally was Bargain Bonanza's new voice-over queen. Her famous line: "Mommy, can I have a Cowboy Cal Kooky Cookie? *Pleeeease?*" was playing on radio and TV stations across the U.S. and Canada. Now she was doing endless variations on the NormalWear slogan: "Fashions for people who are normal. And even those who aren't."

Clara and Laura were modeling selections from the NormalWear collection at locations designed to replicate home, school, and "on the town."

Ben was filming footwear ads, which panicked the rest of us because my brother really *was* a little slow when it came to shoe-tying skills. No matter. The era of shoelaces had officially ended. NormalWear shoes were designed for kids like Ben, who had grown up on Velcro.

Other than posing with my family on a plywood boat for the absurdly small silhouette they used on the NormalWear clothing tags, my schedule was wide open. I credited my Gotta Go performance for this.

The only thing listed next to my name on the November and December schedules was "*Normal* (movie): Creative Consultant." What this meant was that several times a week while the rest of my family was at "work" and I was at the condo reading comic books, I'd get a call from Brandon asking me about our house in Normal, Illinois, or life aboard the S.S. *O'Migosh*.

"We couldn't get a release from Randy Breedlove," Brandon told me one day in early December. He was directing the cast in some early scenes for the movie, which they were filming in Peoria.

"Okay," I said. "Fine with me."

Like I needed the meanest juvenile delinquent at Normal Junior High mad at me.

"So we're making a few changes here and there," Brandon continued. "What I need to know is where you kept the flashlight in your bedroom?"

"The *what*?"

"*Flash*light," he said. "I have you reading your haunted house books under your covers at night, after Ben goes to sleep. So where'd you keep your flashlight?"

"I didn't really use a flashlight," I said. "I just kept the light on. It didn't bother Ben. Or sometimes I'd go in the bathroom and read."

"Okay," Brandon said. "But if you *were* going to read with a flashlight under the covers, wouldn't you keep the flashlight under your bed? So no one would find it?"

"I don't know," I said. "That's not what I did, so I'm not really sure what you're asking."

Muffled sounds in the background. Brandon was talking to someone on the set. "Okay, just forget it," he said. And he hung up.

I made a mental note to tell Sophie about this. Knowing

her low opinion of Brandon made my dealings with him easier.

I declined Brandon's offer to fly me to the film set in Peoria and help on "continuity." I didn't want him to think I was impressed by him. I disliked Brandon, but I wasn't afraid of him. I just didn't want to spend time with him. Not when I could be with Sophie instead.

Okay, so it's not like I was actually *with* her. I just liked going to those Wednesday morning Brand Identity meetings and looking at her. I especially liked when she took off her jacket and I could see her tattoo. *Believe.* I liked wondering what she believed in.

Have I mentioned how pretty Sophie was? Maybe so. But it's worth repeating because it's important. She wasn't cute in that cheerleader way that made you feel so edgy you had to turn away and run. Sophie's beauty was the kind that invited you in and asked you to stay awhile.

And when she smiled her funny, crooked, clown smile, you wanted to laugh and touch her mouth with your finger — just to see what it felt like. Just to see if maybe there was something right there on her lips that you could believe in.

11.

As Christmas approached, I looked forward to finally spending my $1,200. I kept my magazine money in an envelope in the back of my sock drawer. Twelve hundred dollars divided by four siblings and two parents equaled $200 a piece. Perfect. And much neater now that I didn't have to buy a stupid telescope for Charles Goodman.

I asked Mom if I could take a limo to the Galleria, a pricey mall in Dallas with a Saks Fifth Avenue. It was a morning in mid-December when everyone in the family except me was getting ready for a busy day on various Bargain Bonanza sound stages and sets. Mom agreed to let me go shopping alone until I told her my plan to spend the $1,200.

"Save your money, sweetheart," she said. "We're all going Christmas shopping together at Bargain Bonanza. We can get gifts there with our Buckeroos. It won't cost us anything."

My mom. Always the bargain shopper.

A few nights later, my family arrived by limousine at Dallas's new Bargain BIG-Bonanza. We each got our own cart and shopped with our allotment of Bargain Bonanza Buckeroos. When we got back to the condo, we hid the gifts in our closets while two El Rancho bellhops put up a fake Christmas tree in the living room. (Real trees were considered a fire risk at El Rancho.)

On Christmas Eve, Mom insisted we all take naps (*"Naps?!"* Ben shrieked) if we wanted to go to Midnight Mass at the Cathedral Santuario de Guadalupe. But we did, so we did.

Christmas morning found our living room buried in a mountain of plastic packaging and wrapping paper. It was the first time we'd ever exchanged store-bought Christmas presents. Did my family feel empty and unsatisfied by the gross commercialism that replaced what had always been an exquisitely personal and tender exchange of tokens of our affection for one another?

Nope.

"This is the best Christmas *ever!*" Laura announced as she hauled one of many armloads of gifts back to her bedroom.

"No stinkin' *kidding!*" Ben agreed.

I studied Mom and Dad, looking for some trace of disappointment, regret, or even resignation. Nothing. Not even close. They looked tired and older. But they were always tired on Christmas, especially Mom. And they were getting older, after all. We all were.

But that Christmas as we padded around in our Bargain Bonanza pajamas, eating Bargain Bonanza Kampfire Koffee Kake and drinking Very Berry Kranberry Cow Puncher Punch, my mom and dad seemed genuinely happy. This was confirmed later that night when I heard them in the living room. They were sitting on the sofa, watching a fake fire "burn" in the video fireplace.

"Can you believe all this?" Mom said.

"Who would've ever thought?" Dad mused.

I stood in the hallway, listening for clues to what was happening to my family.

"Are you still mad?" Dad asked.

"About what?"

"You know. The taxes."

Silence.

"Yes. No. I don't know. Maybe it all worked out for the best. The kids are loving it."

"I haven't heard anyone complain about homeschool lately," Dad said.

"I know," Mom laughed. "I can barely keep up with their assignments. Even Charles seems happy. We could never have planned this."

When I heard the unmistakable sound of kissing, I skulked down the hallway. *Oh well. At least Mom and Dad were happy*, I thought.

Clara's light was on in her room. She was sitting cross-legged on her bed, drawing. The floor was covered with her Christmas gifts: dozens of new sketch pads and art supplies.

"Hey," she said. She tossed me a Cowboy Cal Kandy Kane from her night table.

"I hate this place," I said, sitting on her dresser next to a stack of used college-entrance exam prep books.

"Why?" she asked.

"It gives me the creeps. Everything's fake. The tree. The fire. The books in the bookcase."

"So," Clara said, not looking up from her sketch pad. "If it's not real, it can't hurt you."

"What are you talking about?" I asked. "Fake things can hurt."

"Name one thing that's not real that can hurt you."

"Okay," I began. "Pretend you're walking in the woods and you see a snake. You think it's a snake, anyway. And you have a heart attack and die. But it turns out it wasn't a snake at all."

"What was it?" Clara asked.

"A stick. Or a rubber snake. Whatever. But it wasn't a real snake, even though you thought it was. And it certainly *did* hurt you because you died."

Clara yawned. "Chums?" she said, her mouth in a wide, twisted shape.

"Yeah?"

"How do you come up with this stuff?"

"Fake snakes?" I said. "Don't tell me you've never thought about having a heart attack about something, and then it turns out it was nothing. Like if someone had a surprise party for you and everybody jumped out and yelled, 'Surprise!' But for one second, your freaked-out brain thinks they're robbers. And you have a heart attack and die. You've never thought how easily you could die from something that's not real? And how embarrassing that would be?"

"Never," she said matter-of-factly. "I'd love someone to throw a surprise party for me." She closed her sketchbook. "Chums, don't assume everyone feels the same way you do."

But of course I did. That was my problem. Or one of them, anyway.

When I returned to my bedroom, I opened my desk drawer and pulled out the only Christmas card I made that year:

Sophie,

Merry Christmas to an abNORMALly good friend. Happy New Year. And please stay out of the men's room.

Chaz
(Charles)

Of course I didn't send it. I didn't know Sophie's home address. Even if I did, I couldn't have sent it. It was obvious from my scratchy-scrawly handwriting that I'd labored for hours over the stupid card, trying to find the right words in the right arrangement to express feelings I still didn't fully understand.

*   *   *

I didn't see Sophie again until the first week in January, when we were in Las Vegas for the launch of Normal-Wear. I told her the What's Next? show reminded me of a World's Fair.

"A World's Fair?" Sophie said, discarding a seven of hearts from her hand. We were playing gin rummy at the Bargain Bonanza booth.

"Yeah," I said. "They used to build these cool attractions, like the Eiffel Tower. That was built for the 1889 World's Fair in Paris."

"How do you know this stuff?" Sophie asked.

"Charles is a brain," said Clara, looking up from Volume II of *All You Need to Know to Ace the PSAT*. She'd brought the book to Las Vegas to work on the vocabulary section. Clara had missed the October PSAT because of a photo shoot for sportswear. Mom rescheduled her to take the test in February.

"A brain, huh?" Sophie said. She snapped her cards in groups of threes on the table. "Well, boy wonder, read 'em and weep."

Though she killed me at cards, Sophie made the launch of NormalWear almost fun. While Laura and Sally collected a suitcase full of promotional giveaways and Ben lost count of how many times he saw the IMAX movie *Adventure on the Atlantic: Treasure! Treason! Terror!*, Sophie, Clara, and I explored the exhibition hall, assigning prizes for the best and worst new products. We gave top honors to Rink-in-a-Room, a linoleum-like material from a Taiwanese carpet manufacturer. You could roll it out over a floor and create an indoor skating rink.

"This would be so perfect for the front hall of the condo," Clara said. "Chums, we should ask Mom if we can get some."

(We did, and she said no. "It's not our house," Mom reminded us.)

Sophie gave the *Is-This-Really-Necessary?* Award to the Incredible Edible Christmas Tree: an eight-foot-tall cookie shaped like a tree and designed to be broken off and eaten for three weeks before Christmas.

"Are they *crazy?*" asked Sophie, chewing on a free sample of the sugary tree. "Who wants a big stale Christmas cookie in their living room? And think of the animals that'll binge themselves to death on this thing. It's just wrong on every level."

I threatened Sophie with the *Meanest-Publicist-In-The-World* Award when she told me about the fashion show.

"It's only two outfits, Charles," she said. "You put on one outfit and walk from here to there." She was pointing to the end of the Willie's Keep On Walkin' Shoes stage. "Then you go backstage and put your second outfit on and do it again."

"Ugh," I said.

Sophie and I were waiting for Clara, who was in line for a free ice-cream cone at a nearby exhibit.

"You know how bad I am at this," I groaned.

The huge mechanized Willie's Keep On Walkin' Shoes began walking around the exhibit hall, as they did every fifteen minutes, accompanied by an annoying jingle. It was fun to watch — once. By the third day, I'd seen the stunt a hundred times and couldn't get the maddening song out of my head.

"How bad you are at *what?*" Sophie asked. "Walking and standing? Because that's all you have to do. Walk, stand, turn, and walk back. There'll be fashion editors in the audience. Some photographers, too. They'll be taking notes and pictures. You don't have to make eye contact with them if you don't want to."

"Ugh," I repeated.

"I'll let you beat me at gin rummy," she offered coyly.

I growled.

"I'll give you a ride on my motorcycle sometime?"

I snarled.

"Okay, will you model just *one* outfit?" she asked.

"Do I *have* to?"

I didn't want to sound like a brat. But I also didn't want to model those dopey Bargain Bonanza clothes.

"Charles," she said, turning to look at me. "If you really, *really* don't want to do this, you don't have to. But you're part of the family, and this whole freakin' clothing line is about you and your family. And I'm afraid if you're not up there, people will ask where you are."

I said nothing.

"I'm willing to negotiate with you on this," she said. "What do you want?"

"I want to meet your son," I said. "James."

It was something that had never crossed my mind until I said it.

She laughed. "Well, *that's* easy enough," she said, shaking my hand formally.

"Where does he stay when you go on trips like this?" I asked.

I could see Clara at the ice-cream exhibit. She was almost to the front of the line.

"With my mom," Sophie said. "You know how grandmas are. Or maybe you don't. Anyway, they have a great time together. She cooks real food, like pot roast and mashed potatoes."

I tried to imagine Sophie's son. I couldn't.

"One outfit," she said.

"It has to be a long-sleeved shirt and long pants. No shorts."

Sophie laughed. "You remind me of me."

"*Really?*" I said. "You seem like the complete opposite of me."

"Why?" she asked. "You think I'm not smart?"

"No," I said. "I know you're smart. But . . ."

"But what?" she said.

"I just picture you being really popular in school. Weren't you one of the popular kids in your class?"

She laughed.

"I don't know if I was *popular*," she said. "Maybe I was. I was like the girls in your magazine story. The mean girls."

"No way," I said. "You weren't like *that*. You were really nice and pretty and cool and —"

Eeps, I thought. *Shut up. I don't want her to know I like her.*

(And please, give me a break. I was fourteen years old. She was beautiful and she was paying attention to me.)

Clara was walking toward us with three ice-cream cones stuck in a cardboard tray.

"I think I *was* sorta mean," Sophie was saying. "But only because I was really insecure when I was young."

"You were insecure?" Clara asked, handing Sophie a chocolate ice-cream cone.

"Yep. Back in high school and junior high."

"See?" Clara said, knocking me in the back with her shoulder and handing me a mint chocolate chip ice-cream cone. "I *told* you you weren't the only one."

I willed myself not to blush.

"Hey, did you guys see those bald people in the orange robes?" Clara asked, licking her sherbet cone as she gestured with her head. "They're chanting."

"Hare Krishnas," Sophie said.

"Serious?" Clara said. We were walking back to the Bargain Bonanza booth.

"Yeah," Sophie said. "They come to this show every year."

"Why would they come to Las Vegas?" I asked. "I thought Hare Krishnas were against gambling."

"They are," said Sophie. "They're also against mass consumerism and materialism. They come to offer an alternative: chanting, dancing, meditation, higher consciousness. All that Hare Krishna stuff. George Harrison was into it for a while."

"Who's George Harrison?" I asked.

Sophie stopped and looked at me. Her eyes were dead serious.

"George Harrison was one of the Beatles, you dope."

"Oh," I said, embarrassed.

"He was the quiet one, right?" Clara said.

"Yeah," Sophie said dreamily. "The shy, spiritual one. George was my favorite Beatle. I had a huge crush on him. Charles, I can't believe you don't know who George Harrison was. What am I going to do with you?"

Just like me, I wanted to say. *Have a crush on me.*

But I didn't. I couldn't. I just made a goofy face and kept walking.

12.

For reasons I will never understand, NormalWear was a huge and immediate success.

"*Fabulous* concept," a British fashion editor said when she stopped by Bargain Bonanza's booth at the What's Next? show.

Sophie knew all of the fashion journalists by first name. When they came to the booth, she pulled them to a corner and talked to them in whispers. She'd say things that elicited big, juicy laughs from the skinny writers, who wrote words like *brave* and *essential* in their black books. As they walked away, Sophie would turn to me, her back to the reporters, and roll her eyes dramatically.

Exactly, I thought. *We're in this together.*

Meanwhile, Dad hated how the Frankly Tools had turned out.

"These are *toys,* not tools," he told Bargain Bonanza's

designers. They explained that the price point they'd been given by Richard meant they'd had to use plastic instead of steel on many of the tools.

Mom liked the sewing projects in her collection, but was uncomfortable endorsing them on TV.

"The thing is, I never use kits like these when I sew," Mom told Sophie before a live segment on *Wake Up, America!* The popular TV morning show was broadcasting from Las Vegas that week, showcasing the hottest new fashions and products.

"I know," said Sophie. "But don't say that on TV. Just say, 'Sewing has always been my favorite way to . . .' What's a sewing word? *Thread?* Sewing is the thread that runs through your life?"

"Can I just say that I like to sew, and I usually make my own patterns?" Mom asked. "Or that I like pretty fabrics?"

"Yeah," said Sophie. "That's good. Sewing is the fabric that threads your family together. Or, you pattern your life around sewing and family. Say whatever you want. Just get Bargain Bonanza in there somewhere."

Mom was a natural. After she taught Cynthia Sanders, the *Wake Up, America!* host, how to make pillowcases from Bargain Bonanza's new Sew You Wanna Sew? kits (with Mom's airbrushed face on the package), Cynthia said: "You know what I love about your family? You're so *real*."

"You think so?" Mom asked.

It got a laugh from Cynthia and the crew, but I know Mom was serious.

Brandon had worked around the clock to get a forty-five-second preview of *Normal*, the movie, ready for the What's Next? show. Sophie convinced the producer of *Wake Up, America!* to show the film clip at the end of the sewing segment. She even wrote suggested copy for Cynthia Sanders, who read it word for word:

"Painful to watch, but ultimately filled with hope, *Normal* promises to be the film this year that captures the nation's imagination while breaking its heart. And before *we* break for a commercial, let's have a sneak peek at *Normal*, due in theaters this April."

The clip was a montage of fast edits and gritty images: a yellow house (not ours), a school (not mine), a child's bike (huh?), the fake *O'Migosh*, and the actors hired to play us. A narrator with a dark, smoky voice read the teaser: "Have you ever been to Normal? If so, you'd know why . . . They Had To Go."

The only glitch was a trio of Hare Krishnas who chanted "Krishna delivers us from the normal ways of the world" while the film clip played. They were still chanting as security guards herded them away.

When we returned to Dallas, Brandon said there was interest in spinning a television series from the movie.

"Focus-group that, Linda," Brandon commanded at the next Brand Identity meeting. "I want to see how a TV series compares to a movie sequel. Outline the demographics for each. And Mark, I want to see a marketing plan pegged to both approaches."

By this time, I could see that Richard was the Brand Identity boss in name only. Brandon was the real leader of this clique. I knew how these things worked. (Remember, I'd attended public school until sixth grade.)

The conference table was littered with newspaper and magazine stories about us. The headlines were predictably silly. "NormalWear Resonates with Normal Shoppers." "Finally — Normal Clothes at Normal Prices." "America: Home of the Free, the Brave, the NORMAL."

The Harrisong Quarterly ("The magazine for people who dream of leaving their normal lives") published its first issue. The feature story was about a family in Brookings, Oregon, who "had taken a page out of the Harrisong family book and left their house in the middle of the night to begin what would be an unforgettable adventure."

Several universities were offering courses based on us. "The Harrisongs: Metaphor for America" was offered in the English Department at Illinois State University. Pace University in New York City had a class called "The S.S. *O'Migosh:* Vehicle for Self-Invention."

Time magazine ran a cover story: "It's Hip to Be Normal." *People* put us on its Valentine's Day cover: "Everyone Loves Normal!" Even the *Wall Street Journal* included the S.S. *Bargain Bonanza,* modeled after the S.S. *O'Migosh,* on its annual What's In list. ("Even if you don't want to live on a houseboat, the easily assembled S.S. *Bargain Bonanza* is fun and kid-friendly. Dock it in the backyard and use as an extra bedroom when relatives visit.")

"It's not about products," Brandon said in an interview with *Advertising Week.* "Normal is a way of life. It's a philosophy."

*　　*　　*

You would've thought by now we'd be rich. And, in fairness, we did live more comfortably (by conventional standards) than we'd ever lived before.

But we never got paid in cash. Twice a month, Richard gave Dad an envelope with a stack of Bargain Bonanza Buckeroos. (Yes, the ones with the picture of a winking Cowboy Cal in the center oval.) Along with the play money, we got a printout with three columns: Hours Worked, Wages Earned, Buckeroos Received.

And so, twice monthly, we dialed *7 from the condo and a limousine driver met us in the lobby of El Rancho and drove us to one of Dallas's countless Bargain Bonanza stores, where we shopped for groceries, socks, batteries — whatever we needed.

Paper towels? We didn't have to reuse them anymore. Shampoo? Go ahead and shampoo, rinse, *and repeat,* as the label instructed. (Mom had always told us the *repeat* cycle was a ploy by shampoo makers to dupe people into wasting their money.)

Still, it's not like we had *everything* we needed or wanted. Bargain Bonanza didn't sell cars. Or houses. Or college educations. I heard Mom worrying about this one night.

"We can't pay the kids' college tuitions with Bargain Bonanza Buckeroos," she was saying to Dad.

"They'll probably *have* Bargain Bonanza colleges in a few years," Dad said. "I know, I know. It's not a joke. I'll talk to Richard. He probably has kids. He'll understand."

Not long after this, Dad told us Bargain Bonanza had agreed to provide private tutors for us, if we wanted them.

"It might be fun," Mom said, wearing her game face.

"I'm sure the tutors are really smart. Some might even be college professors."

The other options were enrolling in public school in Dallas (and being chronically absent because of all the Bargain Bonanza openings we had to attend) or continuing with Mom's more flexible homeschool classes. We all chose Mom, which I know made her feel good.

This was the time I've already described, when Mom began creating word problems based on the number of NormalWear T-shirts worn in this country. The math was still difficult for Laura and Ben. But at least the word problems had some relevance. My brother and sister seemed to take an interest in solving the questions about themselves — as opposed to just guessing wildly.

Encouraged by their progress, Mom asked Ben and Laura to make up their own word problems. I watched Ben scribble his one night in early March, when he and I were sprawled on the sofa in the living room, watching a sitcom on TV.

"If the *acter* playing you in a movie is paid five million dollars and *your* paid in stuff from *Bargin* Bonanza, how fair is that?"

So maybe math wasn't Ben's strong suit. Or spelling, for that matter. But the kid wasn't stupid.

13.

This is where my memory starts to blur. It helps to work backwards.

Richard wanted the release of *Normal,* the movie, to coincide with the launch of the summer line of NormalWear in April. Brandon said *Normal* had to open in New York City on a Friday night. They agreed on April 2, and said we all had to be in New York for the premiere.

"We can't," Mom said at our weekly meeting with the Brand Identity team. "Clara's scheduled to take the PSAT the next morning in Dallas."

Mom was already mad because Clara had missed the February PSAT due to a Valentine's Day photo shoot.

"April third is the last test date this year," Mom said. "She's *not* going to miss it."

"We can get a corporate jet to fly you back to Dallas

after the premiere," Richard said. "We'll have you home by eleven o'clock. And you gain an hour coming home, so it's really ten. That works, right?"

"No," Mom said firmly. "Think how tired she'll be."

"It'll be okay," Clara said, looking at her hands.

"No, it won't," Mom began. "Because —"

"Mom, it's *fine*," Clara whispered, embarrassed. She hated confrontation as much as I did.

Brandon wanted us in New York the day before the premiere for publicity. "Don't look now," he said, "but I think I've got the editors of *That's Style* sold on a cover. This is unprecedented."

Brandon was talking when Sophie sauntered into the meeting, late as usual. She was eating a bagel and carrying a newspaper tucked under her arm.

"Don't look *now*," she said, chewing, "but Alex Randal is one of my best friends. I've been pitching a summer cover to her for months."

"*Alexis Randal?*" Brandon asked. "You know the managing editor of *That's Style?*"

"Yeah," she said, sitting on the window ledge. "Unprecedented, isn't it?"

"Stop it, you two," Richard said. "I don't care who pitched it. Is it going to happen?"

"Sure, why not?" Sophie said. "But they just want Clara. I can go with her early to New York."

"I think *PreTeen Scene* wants to do a video feature on Laura," Brandon said.

"We can do that," Sophie said, boredom written all over her face. Then she turned to Clara and her face brightened. "We can cram for the PSAT when we're in New York. Charles, you should come, too."

My heart did a backflip. *She likes me,* I thought. *She LIKES ME!!!!!!!!!!!!!!!!*

"I want Charlie to bang the opening gavel on Wall Street," Brandon said. "Or ring the bell or whatever."

"Can we get that?" Richard asked.

"We can try," Brandon said. "Right, Sophie?"

But Sophie didn't answer. She was humming faintly and using a pen to punch two holes in her newspaper.

Richard told us that Wall Street analysts had credited the launch of NormalWear with a 52 percent rise in Bargain Bonanza stock. Our clothing and lifestyle products were breaking ridiculous records.

"I want Charlie on Wall Street, Clara on the cover of *That's Style,* Laura on *PreTeen Scene,* and everyone at the premiere," Brandon directed. He looked like the commander of a military operation. "And I want one of our photographers at the *That's Style* shoot so we have fresh photos of the NormalWear summer line for the premiere on Friday night."

"Whatever," Sophie said as she rolled her beautifully bored eyes across the ceiling. Then she held the newspaper up to her face and turned toward me. Only her eyes peeked out from the holes she'd punched in the paper.

It made me laugh. It was silly and stupid, but for some reason it gave me joy. It made me feel strange and wonderful.

*   *   *

Sophie, Clara, Laura, and I flew to New York on Thursday afternoon. The day before we left, I tried to talk Sophie into bringing her son with us.

"No, no," she said. "He and his grammy already have plans. She's helping him with some science fair project."

"I could help him with that," I said. But the instant the words tumbled out, I realized how pathetically Ben-ish I sounded. So I let it drop.

We were booked at the Hotel Plaza Athénée. Laura said it looked like an old, fancy candy box. After we dropped off our bags, we went by cab to dinner at a tiny place in Chinatown with blood-red walls.

"This is so fun!" Laura gushed, using her fingers to wrap lo mein noodles around her chopsticks. "I *love* New York."

"Me too," Sophie said. "I want to make sure we have time to go to MoMA after the photo and video shoots tomorrow."

"*Moma?*" Clara asked.

"The Museum of Modern Art," Sophie explained. "You'll love it. And Charles, I want you to see the New York Public Library and Central Park and . . . well, just everything."

Sophie knew all about New York. She'd lived there after she graduated from college. She said she had a million things she wanted to show us.

"Let's think," she said. "Clara has to be at her photo shoot at nine. Laura, a crew is picking you up in the lobby at ten for the video shoot. Charles has to be at the stock exchange at seven thirty, so you should leave the hotel at seven."

We were back at the hotel, sitting on the floor in Sophie's room. (Regrettably, her suite was on the sixteenth floor, two floors above ours.)

"You don't have to come with me," I said, knowing Sophie hated getting up early.

"No, no," Sophie said. "It'll be good for me. We'll meet in the lobby at seven and go to your thing. Then we'll go to Clara's photo shoot and Laura's. Then we'll have all afternoon to do whatever we want. We'll meet up with the rest of your family for dinner."

She was counting out a hundred dollars in "walking around" money for Clara, Laura, and me.

"This is Manhattan," Sophie said, handing me a stack of tens and twenties. "Bargain Bonanza Buckeroos don't cut it here."

Though shopping held no appeal for me, the idea of spending an entire day with Sophie made me so giddy, I didn't sleep more than an hour that night. But the next morning at seven, Sophie wasn't in the lobby. I took the elevator to her room. A DO NOT DISTURB sign hung on the doorknob. I knocked gently. No answer. So I let her sleep.

Luckily, a reporter and photographer from *This Week in America* were in the lobby. We shared a cab to Wall Street.

Going through security at the New York Stock Exchange took longer than the actual bell ringing, which lasted all of five seconds. I tried to fake a smile for the photographers, but I was never good at that. When a *New York Times* photographer told me to stop wincing, I asked someone to show me where the exit was and left.

I didn't know where Laura's and Clara's photo shoots were, and I didn't feel like going back to the hotel. So I wandered the streets of Manhattan alone.

I found I had a strange kind of courage that day. I had hoped to be with Sophie, but I enjoyed the freedom to think about her in a way that I couldn't when she was there. Without her, I could replay our conversations and mentally rewrite them, always improving my parts, making me wittier and more mature.

I bought a pretzel and a map from a sidewalk vendor and set off in search of the New York Public Library. I must've walked right past it. When I finally stopped and asked, a man told me to turn around and walk six blocks back.

"Look for the stone lions in front," he said.

I found the library and went inside. I roamed happily up and down the narrow, church-like aisles. I almost laughed when I found myself surrounded by philosophy books. I pulled a dark blue book from the shelf. It was titled *The Complete Writings of Georg Wilhelm Friedrich Hegel.* I opened it to a random page.

> *Genuine tragedy is a case not of right against wrong but of right against right.*

I read the sentence several times, but couldn't force my brain to decipher its meaning. I turned to another page and read:

> *The only way a conflict between right and right can end is with the death of one side or the other.*

It was too hard. My mind was somewhere else. I replaced the book on the shelf. On the way out of the library, I found a free, cartooned brochure about the stone lions. I went outside and read it.

— The Cats' Meow —

The famous felines that stand guard in front of the New York Public Library were sculpted by Edward Clark Potter from pink Tennessee marble. On duty since 1911, the lions' nicknames have changed over the years. At first they were called Leo Astor and Leo Lenox, after the founders of the library. Later, they were known as Lord Astor and Lady Lenox. Today we call them Patience and Fortitude, the nicknames given to the lions during the 1930s by New York Mayor Fiorello LaGuardia. He said Patience and Fortitude were the qualities New Yorkers needed to survive the economic depression.

I started to walk away from the library, then turned back and waved at the lions.

I can't explain what made me do it or how I felt that day other than to say I was happy and alive in a way I don't think I'd ever been before. Everything felt so big and bright. It made me feel like a different, better version of myself; like how I'd always imagined Clara must feel — secretly hoping someone, somewhere was planning a surprise party for her.

It was after five o'clock by the time I finally got back to the hotel. The rest of my family had arrived, as evidenced by Ben's luggage in my room and a note on my bed:

Early Dinner at 5 p.m. In Hotel Restaurant.
Meet us there. Shirt with a collar, please.
                    Dad

I changed my clothes and went downstairs. Mom, Dad, Ben, Laura, and Sally were already eating.

"Where's Clara?" I asked, looking at a menu.

"She doesn't feel well," Mom said.

I ordered a bowl of clam chowder. I hadn't eaten anything all day other than the pretzel.

"This is the coolest city in the world," I said. "I saw everything. Rockefeller Center. The Empire State Building. The New York Public Library. There are these two big stone lions in front of it. Their names are Patience and Fortitude. They're called that because —"

"Was Sophie with you today?" Dad asked. He was mad.

"No," I said, looking from Dad to Laura. "I thought she was with you guys."

Laura shook her head. She was eating a piece of cheesecake. "She never came to my photo shoot — or Clara's," Laura said.

Oh God!

"I'll go check on her," I said, getting up from the table.

"Wait for your soup," Mom ordered.

My soup? When Sophie could be dead in her room?

"I'm not hungry," I said, dropping my red cloth napkin on the table.

The DO NOT DISTURB sign was gone. I knocked.

"Sophie?" I said. "Sophie."

I knocked harder. She opened the door on the sixth knock.

"Hey," she said. She was wearing a white hotel bathrobe. "Come in. How'd it go today?"

"Oh," I said, exhaling. "I was worried about you."

She laughed. I could smell her perfume.

"I'm the one who's supposed to worry about you," she said. "Sorry I missed the Wall Street thing this morning. Was it okay?"

I sat on her bed and watched her brush her hair in front of the mirror.

"Yeah, it was fine. And the library here is so cool!"

"I knew you'd love that," she said, looking at her reflection. "How'd Clara and Laura's photo shoots go?"

"They did fine," I said, trying to breathe in the smell of her perfume. "Clara's not feeling well."

My eyes were scanning her room. She had fifteen or twenty shopping bags strewn on the bed and floor. Shopping. Sophie'd been shopping all day. Well, that was okay. She's a girl. Of course she liked to shop. Of course I didn't expect her to hang out with me in New York City.

(Of course I'm lying.)

"She doesn't feel well?" Sophie said, now brushing makeup over her eyelids. "Does she feel okay enough to go to the premiere?"

"I don't know," I said. "We haven't talked today."

I poked my head in one of the bags on the floor. Shoes.

Sophie swatted my hand playfully. "Don't snoop," she said. "Go tell Clara we need her at the premiere. She's the ingénue. The show can't go on without her."

Now Sophie was applying mascara to her eyelashes. I couldn't take my eyes off her.

"Go tell her," she said.

"I like your hair like that," I said.

She made a face in the mirror. "What's wrong with my hair?"

"Nothing." I said. "It's just, I don't know, fluffier or something, right?"

"If you must know, I had it done today," she said, admiring her mane in the mirror. Then she turned to look at me: *"Go."*

"Okay, I'm going."

I didn't move from the bed. (*God, what an idiot I was.*)

"I like those earrings, too," I said.

"Charles!"

"Okay, okay. I'm going."

I hunched over and began humming the jingle from the Willie's Keep On Walkin' Shoes exhibit as I did my best imitation of a robotic walking shoe. I walked out of her room that way.

Halfway down the hall, I could still hear Sophie's wonderful laugh.

14.

I floated down to the fourteenth floor and knocked on Clara's door.

"Who is it?" she asked.

"Me. Charles."

I listened impatiently to the heavy *clumpclumpclump* as Clara made her way to the door and let me in. The unmistakable smell of vomit clung to the room.

"Sorry you're sick," I said.

"Me too," she said, crawling back into bed. She had a pot of tea on the night table.

"Flu?" I asked.

"Mom thinks it might be food poisoning," Clara said.

"Yuck. From what?"

"The food at the photo shoot today," she said. "Bad chicken salad or something."

"How'd it go — besides that?" I asked.

Clara shook her head and groaned. Her hair was a frizzy mess.

"The summer line is really stupid," she said. "Stupid clothes, stupid slogan. I want to go home."

I thought she meant the condo in Dallas.

"I miss the water," she continued. "I miss the *O'Migosh*."

"Yeah," I said. Then I paused. I wanted to seem sympathetic. "Sophie wanted to make sure you're well enough to go to the premiere tonight."

"Like I have a choice," Clara said.

This wasn't like Clara. She was never sarcastic.

"If you're really sick," I said, "you don't have to go."

"Of course I'm *really* sick," she snapped. "Why would I pretend to be sick?"

"Sorry," I said, equally sarcastic.

There was a brand-new PSAT study guide on her bed and a yellow legal pad. I could see Clara's handwriting on the top page.

"What're you writing?" I asked, trying to read it.

"Nothing." She tore off the page and crumpled it up in a ball.

"Sheesh. Someone's in a bad mood."

Clara's eyes filled with tears.

"What's wrong with you?" I said.

But even I could hear the sharp tone of impatience in my voice. I tried again. "What."

"On top of everything else," she began, "I just found out there's a writing section on the PSAT."

"So."

"Chums, I can't write. You know I can't write."

Who was this girl? Clara could do anything.

"It's a stupid creative writing thing," she said, blowing her nose in a washcloth. "It's new this year. I have to, like, make up a story. On the spot."

"Make it up before you go," I said. "Have an outline. A plan."

"I'm not good at that!" she said.

"It's easy," I started. "Just pick a —"

"You're not helping!" she yelled, throwing a pillow at me. "Go away."

Fine. I had better things to do.

I left Clara's room and went down the hall to my room to get dressed for the premiere — and to think about Sophie Buchanan in her white bathrobe.

*   *   *

When she saw me an hour later in the hotel lobby, Sophie burst out laughing.

"Now *that's* hideous," she said.

She was pointing at my mock tuxedo made from sweat-suit material. Mark in Marketing had told us what we had to wear to the premiere. My outfit was from Bargain Bonanza's spring line called NormalFormal. Even the shoes were ridiculous: black satin high-top tennis shoes covered in sparkles.

"I know," I said. "Wow, you look great."

She was wearing a sapphire blue dress with a matching scarf wrapped around her shoulders. She looked amazing.

"Thanks, sweetie," Sophie said. Then she turned to Clara: "How can you be so pretty even when you're sick?"

Clara just shrugged.

Sophie rode with my family in a limo to the premiere. Brandon, Richard, Mark, and Iris were waiting for us, along with dozens of reporters and photographers, by a red carpet.

"I thought the red carpet was just in the movies," Laura cooed in a stage whisper.

"Well, kiddo, this *is* the movies," Brandon said loud enough for the reporters to hear.

As we stood on our assigned tape marks on the red carpet, I listened to Angela Andrews, the celebrity reporter from *Entertainment Exclusive.*

"For months, the Harrisongs have been making America feel *good* about being normal," Angela said to the camera.

"This weekend, the movie based on the famous family from Normal opens in theaters across America. With the release of the movie *Normal,* Bargain Bonanza is taking a bold step and introducing its summer line of clothes called SexyNormal. Because it's normal to be sexy, and it's sexy to be normal."

The camera operator was now standing directly in front of us. Angela Andrews held a microphone in front of my dad's face.

"Frank, after this break, I'm going to ask you how you like the new ad campaign, and especially these very sexy pictures of your oldest daughter."

I watched Angela Andrews's white-tipped fingers open a Bargain Bonanza press kit and pull out glossy photos of Clara.

"She looks terrific," Angela said, fanning the photos in front of us.

Mom gasped. I think I did, too. The photos were like something out of the *Victoria's Secret* catalog: close-up shots of Clara in skimpy bathing suits that left little to the imagination. In some of the pictures, Clara was looking away with a misty expression on her face. In other pictures, she looked directly at the camera with pouty lips and way too much makeup.

What was she thinking?

"Those swimming suits don't even fit you," Mom hissed.

"I know," Clara said. "I look stupid."

Not according to the male photographers.

"Clara, this way!" they cackled. "Clara, say 'sexy'!"

"We're back," Angela Andrews announced. "Clara, before I ask your dad how he feels about the new advertising campaign, let me ask you: In what way do you think it's normal to be sexy, and sexy to be normal?"

"I don't know," Clara said softly, looking at her shoes.

Brandon interrupted. "Well, it's certainly normal to be nervous on the night of your premiere, isn't it?"

He sounded like a game show host. I noticed he'd replaced the gold stud in his ear with a small hoop.

All I could think as we were shown to our seats was how Mom and Dad were going to filet Clara for posing like that. But not until after the movie. Clara had the advantage of Mom's and Dad's tempers cooling a bit before she got in trouble. Maybe the movie would provide a nice diversion. I hoped Clara's pictures hadn't ruined it for them. I wanted Mom and Dad to enjoy our weird celebrity.

When the lights went down, I felt the old familiar swing set in my stomach. Only then did I realize how awful the movie could be.

In no particular order: Dad was portrayed as a small-town crook who did odd jobs in order to gain access to people's homes, where he pursued his *real* job of stealing jewelry, wallets, piggy banks (!), and basically anything he could fit in his toolbox. Mom's character was clueless to her husband's shenanigans — maybe because she was too busy sweetening her iced tea with some mysterious elixir from the liquor cabinet. (Mom, who I never saw drink anything other than Communion wine at Mass.)

The actress who played Laura was an unlikable little brat. The audience actually cheered when she fell while learning to ride a bike. Sally had zero lines. She was an infant, simply an appendage to Mom's hip.

Clara, meanwhile, was a hippie flake. Ben had some sort of condition that made him laugh like a fool while he slurped spaghetti straight from his plate, like a dog.

My character was humorless and pious, turning and speaking directly to the camera at several points in the drama. ("As you can see, I felt like an outsider, even inside the four walls of my house.")

A half hour into the movie, I had to go. To the bathroom, of course. From there I could hear the audience's muffled laughter. Then the collective gasps. More laughter.

I sat on the toilet, staring at my Little Benny watch, wishing the night would end.

I was waiting in the back of the theater when the audience began trickling out in groups of twos and threes. *"Wasn't it amazing? That school scene: gut-wrenching! I loved it. Didn't you just love it? And those white doves at the end, leading the O'Migosh to safety and happiness. Sooooo sweet!"*

I knew something was wrong when I saw Dad charging down the aisle.

"Come on," he yelled at me. "Get in the limo."

I was right. I knew Clara was going to get in trouble for posing like that in those pictures. I was just surprised that Dad had maintained his level of fury during the movie.

Dad was elbowing reporters out of the way.

"Move!" he yelled, pushing Ben in the limo.

Oh, so it was Ben. *Figures.* He must've misbehaved during the movie. Whatever Ben had done in there had been bad. Dad's face was bright red. Clara was crying. Mom looked shell-shocked.

"What happened?" I asked Mom as she slid in the limo next to me.

"Clara," she whispered.

I looked at Clara. Was it something besides the photos?

"*What?*" I said.

Clara just shook her head and looked out the window.

Dad was yelling something at a reporter. Then he climbed in the limo.

"Go!" Dad told the driver.

Everyone in the backseat was silent.

"Okay, so don't tell me," I mumbled.

I looked out the window, hoping for a glimpse of Sophie. A crowd of moviegoers was clustered around a guy selling rabbits and white turtledoves wearing ridiculously tiny SexyNormal T-shirts.

I didn't care about that. I wanted to see Sophie again in her blue dress. It wasn't really the color of sapphires. It was more like the color of a Siamese cat's eyes. Or the Gulf of Mexico at night.

I wondered if I could get up the courage to tell her she looked like a goddess. Sophia: the goddess of wisdom. Probably not. But at least we could laugh about how stupid the movie was, how stupid Brandon was, how he'd ruined my story, my wonderful story, the story of a good-intentioned boy who —

"Clara got pregnant," Mom whispered in my ear.

15.

I was struck dumb. I couldn't even form a question until we got back to the hotel.

"*Pregnant?*" I asked Dad. "How? Who?"

He was sitting on the bed in his and Mom's suite. He didn't answer.

"Dad, *tell* me. Please."

"That Randy Breedlove kid," he said, rubbing his forehead.

"What are you talking about?" I said. "Clara hasn't even seen him since junior high in Normal."

"In the movie. Clara gets pregnant."

I laughed with relief.

"You mean she was just pregnant in the *movie?*" I said. "I thought you meant she was really pregnant."

He looked at me in disgust. "Get out of here."

"But, Dad —"

"Get OUT."

Mom was standing in the hallway with Sally.

"I'm not a baby," Sally said, sobbing.

"I know," Mom said, turning to look at me. "That was a silly movie, wasn't it?"

"But I'm *not* a baby," Sally continued.

"That wasn't us, sweetheart," Mom said. "That was a whole different family."

"But they had *our* names," Sally cried.

"I know," Mom said. "Wasn't that silly?"

Mom stared at me. I kept walking toward my room.

"Charles," she said. Her voice was expressionless.

"Yeah?"

"We're not going back to Dallas tonight," Mom said. "It's too late. We're leaving in the morning."

That meant Clara would miss the PSAT again.

"Okay," I said.

Laura came out of her and Clara's room. She was holding a can of Cowboy Cal Cola and glaring at me.

"Now everyone in the world will think I'm a brat," she said. "Thanks to *you*."

"Laura," I began, "I didn't have anything to do with —"

"You did *so!*" she snarled. "You're a big fat liar. You hate us all. Well, fine. I hated you first." She turned and slammed the door.

I swiped my key down the electronic lock outside my room. The door opened, revealing a silhouette of Ben sitting on the bed he'd claimed. He was watching soccer on TV.

"What a disaster, huh?" I said, walking toward his bed.

Ben stared at the television.

"I mean, they got everything wrong," I soldiered on. "Every single thing."

He didn't respond.

"Ben," I said, sitting next to him on the bed.

He turned away. "You think I'm stupid, don't you?" he said to the wall.

"Of course I don't."

"Yeah, you do," he said. "You've always thought that."

I got up from the bed and positioned myself between Ben and the wall. His eyes were wet.

"Ben," I said, touching his shoulders lightly. He flinched.

"Don't touch me!" he hissed. "I'm not *smart* enough for you." He turned and stared at the television with a blank expression.

"That's not what I think," I said. "Or how I feel."

"Oh, yeah?" he said, now standing. He marched to the luggage rack in the corner that held my suitcase. He began throwing my clothes on the floor.

"*This* is how I feel," he said, his eyes focused on the growing pile of clothes on the floor. "This is how *everybody* feels about you. Clara, too."

Clara was confiding in Ben? When did this start?

My legs felt wobbly as I stumbled down the hallway toward Laura and Clara's room. I needed to tell Clara something. But what? That none of this was real? That this was all just a fake snake in the woods?

I should've, but I didn't. I couldn't. Instead, I ran toward the elevators. I pressed the button frantically — UP, UP, UP — until the elevator arrived with a dismissive *pling*.

When I got to the sixteenth floor, I sprinted to Sophie's room and pounded on the door.

"Sophie!" I yelled. "Sophie!"

No answer. I kept pounding on the door. *Where was she?*

Then I heard her unmistakable laugh. She was getting off the elevator. I ran toward her voice, but stopped when I saw Brandon. He had his arm wrapped tightly around Sophie's waist. He was kissing her neck. She was kissing him back.

Of course. Of course. Of course.

It was one of those moments when you know your life is changing in ways that will forever affect who you are.

(And please. I know it was the most obvious thing in the world, but I didn't see it. Not until I saw it and felt it with my own gut. That's where I felt it first: my gut.)

I ran past Sophie and Brandon toward a door marked EMERGENCY EXIT. I was in a stairwell. I ran two flights up. I heard the door open below me.

"Charles?"

It was Sophie. She was alone.

"Charles?" she repeated.

I didn't respond. I just stood there, still as a statue.

"Did you hate the movie?" she yelled. "It was even worse than we expected, wasn't it, sweetie? I was just telling Brandon how much I hated it."

She was slurring her words. Was she drunk?

"Charles, come talk to me," she said.

I leaned my head over the stair rail. She had her scarf tied around her waist, revealing her bare arms and tattoo. She saw me above her.

"Come here, you," she said.

I know it was stupid, but I needed her. I needed to be with her. I walked down the stairs. The sparkles were already coming off my NormalFormal tennis shoes.

"Wasn't it awful?" she said, holding out both hands. "What a bunch of crap, huh?"

My eyes were burning.

"I can't believe what they did to Ben," I said. "Making him a lamebrain. And Clara."

But I was lying. I wasn't thinking about them at all. I was thinking about me. I was thinking: *I can't believe what you're doing to me. Don't do this to me. Don't be a mean girl.*

"Subtlety is not Brandon's hallmark," Sophie said. The bright light made her look old and garish.

The emergency exit door opened. It was Brandon.

"We were just talking about you and your stupid movie," Sophie yelled at him. She was laughing. "Charles, go ahead. You won't hurt Brandon's feelings."

I couldn't think of anything to say. I was back in sixth grade. I was paralyzed by this clique leader and his beautiful girlfriend. I thought everything had changed. But nothing had. Something was always *always* breaking.

"I obviously had to make some changes to your material," Brandon said. "I know that's always hard for the writer."

At least he was acknowledging I was a writer.

Sophie began gesturing wildly with her hands. "Charles

has more talent in his little finger than you have in your whole —"

She almost fell down the steps. Brandon caught her. God, she was a mess.

"What's cool," Brandon said, "is where we can go from here." He was ignoring Sophie now and talking directly to me. "It's the perfect place to launch the TV series. And I already know who I want to adopt Clara's baby. Mrs. Hannigan, the librarian."

"You mean Mrs. *Flanagan?*" I asked.

"Yeah," he said. "Hannigan. Flanagan. Whatever."

He got it all wrong. And he didn't even care.

As far as I knew, Clara had never even kissed a boy. Randy Breedlove, on the other hand, was *doing it* (as they said) before he could do long division. I tried to explain this to Brandon.

"The girl Randy Breedlove got pregnant wasn't Clara," I said. "She was an eighth grader. Her name was Lacy Montjoy."

I felt a pang of guilt as soon as I said it — as if that poor girl hadn't suffered enough. As if I had any business telling Brandon her name. I won a point of logic by compromising Lacy Montjoy's right to privacy.

Brandon just laughed. "Lacy Montjoy? I wish you'd told me. I would've used that."

I felt dizzy and not really there.

Sophie was hiccupping. She *was* drunk. How could she have let this happen? Why wasn't she at the photo shoot? Because she was shopping. For herself. That's what she believed in.

"You wouldn't've let this happen to James," I whispered to Sophie. "You'd take better care of him."

"*James?*" Brandon asked. "Who's James?"

"Her son," I said, not even looking at Brandon.

"Sophie with kids?" Brandon laughed. "Now that's good. You told Charlie you have a son?"

"Mmm-hmmm," Sophie said. "I want a kid."

"You don't have a son?" I asked.

"No, honey," Sophie slurred. "I said I *wanted* one."

And there it was, just like that. A sharp little truth with edges like blades. I knew in that moment that God hated me.

I looked at Brandon and Sophie. Then I ran. When I heard them laughing, I ran faster. Hot tears were filling my eyes and blurring my vision. I felt the kaleidoscope that was my life turning, revealing an entirely new pattern of shapes and colors. Or maybe it was showing me the pattern that was always there, waiting for me to see it.

16.

Dad had a different response.

At LaGuardia Airport the next morning, when a reporter asked how it felt to have such a "hot" daughter, Dad punched him. When a photographer took a picture of him hitting the reporter, Dad slugged him, too.

"Leave my family *alone!*" he yelled.

But that only encouraged the photographers and reporters, who suddenly had a story on their hands.

Dad was still swinging when airport security handcuffed him. We waited four and a half hours while he was questioned in a back office.

I found a discarded copy of *The New York Times* on a plastic chair. The lead story in the business section was titled "Bargain Bonanza Gets Sexy." Under the headline were pictures of Clara in skimpy swimsuits. I read the first few paragraphs:

Riding on the heels of the phenomenally successful NormalWear line of clothing and lifestyle products, Bargain Bonanza is introducing a sexy collection of summer clothes for the whole family.

The print campaign features Clara Harrisong wearing — barely — the discount giant's new line of swimwear and purring the seductive mantra "It's normal to be sexy. And it's sexy to be normal."

At sixteen, Clara is the oldest of the five happy-go-lucky Harrisong children, who, along with their parents, went from living on a moldy houseboat to living the American dream. Now a household name, the Harrisongs are enjoying a level of celebrity normally reserved for Hollywood stars.

Clara saw me reading the article.

"Want to take a walk?" I asked, folding the newspaper and stuffing it in a metal garbage can.

We walked for more than two hours, making giant loops around the A, B, and C terminals. She told me about the *That's Style* shoot.

"I'm a size eight," Clara said. "But they only had size-four swimming suits."

I groaned.

"And they gave me champagne," she said. "They said it would loosen me up."

I remembered my Gotta Go fiasco and the sodium

concoction Crystal gave me to drink. I should've warned Clara. I should've been paying attention.

"And then the bad chicken salad on top of it," I said.

"The food never showed up," Clara said.

"What?"

"There was no chicken salad. I made that up. There was no food at all. Just champagne. Lots of it. That's probably why I got sick."

"Why didn't you tell Mom and Dad?"

"I didn't want them to get mad at me."

"They wouldn't have gotten mad at *you*," I said.

"I should've known not to drink," she said. "It was my fault."

"No, it wasn't," I said.

My mind and body felt disconnected. I kept forgetting to swallow. Sometimes I forgot to breathe. I had to remind myself of the facts: I was walking through a New York City airport. I was waiting for Dad to be released from security. My sister's picture was in the newspaper. She was wearing (barely) swimsuits.

We had come so far from Normal.

"Poor Ben," Clara was saying. "He's really upset they made him . . . you know, *slow*."

She looked at me. We burst out laughing.

"It's not funny," Clara said, covering her mouth. "There's nothing funny about it."

"But it's just so ridiculous," I replied. "For them to make him like that in the movie. But also for him to be *upset* by it. The whole thing is just crazy. It's not real at all."

"I know," she said.

I thought about bringing up Clara's pregnancy in the movie. But I couldn't. Making Clara pregnant was just as ridiculous as making Ben dimwitted, but there was something darker in Clara's case. I couldn't go there.

"And I hate that they made Dad out to be a thief," Clara said. "He's the most honest man in the world."

I took a breath. *Should I tell her?*

Before I could think about it, I found myself telling Clara how Lawrence Leech and Alan Grayson had used Dad's failure to file tax returns as blackmail to get Mom and Dad to sign the contract with Bargain Bonanza.

"*Tax evasion?*" she said. "That's what this was all about? Why didn't you tell me."

"Dad asked me not to."

We walked in silence for a few minutes.

"Chums," she said. "Dad's not a real criminal. He's just disorganized about paperwork and stuff, right?"

"People do things every day worse than what he did," I said.

I stopped walking. I had to ask her.

"Did you know Brandon and Sophie were . . . boyfriend and girlfriend?"

"I didn't *know* know," Clara said.

"But you knew?"

"It was sorta obvious," she said. "From the way they flirted during the meetings."

That was flirting? Why was I such an idiot?

"You should've told me," I grumbled.

"*Really?*" she said. "I thought it was totally obvious. Sorry, Chums."

"No, if anyone should be apologizing, it's me," I said. "Everything's my fault. I never should've written that stupid magazine story. Or I should've gone to Peoria while they were filming. Now everyone's mad at me and —"

"No one's mad at you," Clara said. "I told the little kids this morning that you had nothing to do with the movie."

"Thanks," I mumbled. "I owe you."

"Then get us out of this," Clara said.

"You mean New York?"

"No, this." Clara waved her hand in a circle.

I knew what she meant. All of it. The whole ugly mess.

"But Mom and Dad signed a legal contract," I said. "We can't get out of it. Bargain Bonanza has the right to make us do this stuff."

"But what about *our* rights?" Clara asked. "Don't we have the right not to be so . . . *used?*"

I stopped walking.

"What is it, Chums?"

"One side has to die," I said.

"*What?*"

"The only way a conflict between right and right can end is with the death of one side or the other," I said, remembering Hegel's words that I'd read the day before in the New York Public Library.

"Chums, you're scaring me," she said.

"It's so obvious," I said. "It won't even be that hard."

And so began my Hegelian plan.

17.

We were summoned to an emergency Brand Identity meeting on Monday.

"This new image is fantastic," said Brandon. He was holding a copy of the *New York Post*. The headline on the front page read: "Frank Harrisong Lashes Out: 'It's Normal to Feel Protective,' Say Shrinks."

"What can we do with it?" Iris in Asia asked enthusiastically.

"Whatever it is, we've gotta move fast," said Brandon.

"I've got it!" Mark in Marketing erupted. "Home security products."

"And men's fragrance," said Richard. "Call it The Protector. Evoke the musky smell of an animal protecting his young."

"How dare you," Dad said, slowly rising out of his chair. "How dare *all* of you."

Before anyone could stop him, Dad had Richard by the collar.

"You think this is a *game?*" Dad demanded. "Do you? *DO* you? Do you think we're just dolls or dogs you can dress up in little *costumes* to sell your worthless Bargain Bonanza —"

"Whoa," Richard said. He turned to Mark. "Call security."

"We don't need security," Dad yelled, throwing Richard against the wall. "I just need you to stop telling me and my family what to —"

Alan Grayson was suddenly at the door.

"Is there a problem here?" Grayson asked, gliding in the room.

Dad released his hands from around Richard's neck.

"Sorta," Richard said, coughing. "Frank here didn't like the idea of the fragrance line I was telling you about this morning. Which is fine. We can think of something else to do with this new development."

"You have no right," Dad said. "No right at all."

"Actually, we have every right," Grayson said.

Clara looked at me and raised her eyebrows.

Five minutes later, after Bargain Bonanza security guards had taken Dad to cool off, Sophie strolled in, tardy as usual. I didn't look at her.

With Dad gone, the room went quiet.

"You guys have been putting in such long days," Brandon finally said, breaking the awkward silence. "Know what I think you need? Some time off. They don't have anything they absolutely *have* to do this week, do they? Sophie, do you have anything for them?"

"No," she said, getting up to feed the birds.

Fine. I'm not looking at you, either.

"Then take some time off," Brandon said. "Right, Richard? They should take some time off. A week. Two weeks?"

Richard was still looking at his torn collar and frowning.

"Yeah," he said. "Whatever."

*　　*　　*

We spent the rest of the week in the condo. It was the first real vacation we'd had since we'd arrived in Dallas. But it was hardly relaxing. Dad stomped around the house, kicking furniture, breaking (on accident, he said) at least three coffee mugs.

I overheard pieces of Mom and Dad's conversations.

"You need to calm down," Mom was saying. "There's not much we can do about this right now."

"The hell there isn't," Dad barked.

While the little kids watched daytime TV, I took a cordless phone into Clara's bedroom. We'd spent the previous afternoon at the Dallas Public Library, researching the Internal Revenue Service and its policy on tax evaders.

"The IRS generally looks with favor upon those who come forward voluntarily," I told Clara, reading from my notes. "You just have to go in and say you didn't pay your taxes for whatever reason. But that you want to make it up. And then you work out a plan to pay them back. It's called *amnesty*."

"How much do you think we owe?" Clara asked.

"I don't know. We've got to call."

I tapped out the numbers for the Dallas IRS office.

"Hello?" I said to the woman who answered the phone. "I . . . I want to take advantage of your amnesty program."

"You'll need to make an appointment to come talk with an agent," she said.

"But I . . . I'm handicapped," I said. "I'm autistic. . . . No, not artistic. *Au*tistic."

Clara held her hand over her mouth to stifle her laughter.

"I have autism," I continued. "All I know is that I haven't paid my taxes for the last few years and I want to settle up. I just need to know how much I owe."

"What's your Social Security number?" she asked.

I had no idea. I told the women I'd call her back.

Clara found Mom's and Dad's Social Security numbers

the next morning by asking when she could get her driver's license, and then begging Mom and Dad to show her their licenses.

We called the IRS back that afternoon. I got a crabby agent this time, who said she couldn't talk about the amnesty program over the phone.

Clara took the phone and hit the redial button.

"I'm going to have a baby," Clara said into the phone. "Next week. That's right. And my husband and I want to get our tax situation cleared up before the baby arrives. Well, wouldn't you? So, look, if I tell you our Social Security numbers, and give you the best estimate on how much money we made over the past five years, can you tell me how much we owe?"

In less than one minute, we learned that our parents owed $4,357.

"That's nothing," whispered Clara.

"I know," I said. "But I don't think the IRS takes Bargain Bonanza Buckeroos. I've still got my magazine money. That's $1,200."

"No," said Clara. "Save that."

She picked up the phone and pressed *7.

"We need a limo, please," she said. "Two passengers to Bargain BIG-Bonanza."

18.

"You're going to Bargain BIG-Bonanza *again?*" Mom asked one afternoon, weeks later, when she heard Clara call for a limo.

"Do you mind?" Clara asked.

"No, I don't *mind,*" Mom said. "But I don't know why you two can't remember to get what you need when we all go shopping together on Sundays after church."

Well, because what we *needed* was $4,357 in Bargain Bonanza crap that we could take to pawn shops and sell for cash.

It was Clara's idea to use pawn shops to convert our Bargain Bonanza plunder into real money. There was no shortage of Bargain Bonanza Buckeroos. We had two drawers in the kitchen stuffed with the cartoon currency.

But it took dozens of shopping trips to collect enough watches, jewelry, DVDs, and small electronics. We always told the limo drivers we wanted to walk back to the condo. That's how we found Dallas's best pawn shops.

It was the middle of May now, a full year since my stupid magazine story had appeared in *Modern Times*. Dallas was hot and muggy, but it felt good to walk outside with Clara, even though she had to wear big sunglasses and a hat. Otherwise, she'd be mobbed by fans asking for her autograph. Her swimsuit pictures were on every bus in town.

Only a few people recognized me from the Gotta Go commercials. Those who did were usually too embarrassed to admit it.

The day we went to the IRS office, I asked Clara to wait in the ladies' room. We couldn't take a chance of someone recognizing her.

"My mom recently had a baby," I told the IRS agent. "I think you spoke with her on the phone? She asked me to deliver this to you."

The woman yawned as I handed her three plastic pencil pouches from the NormalWear line of school supplies.

"You're paying in *cash?*" she asked, unzipping the first pouch. She was suddenly alert.

"We don't have a bank account," I said truthfully. "Can I have a receipt for our payment, please?"

The woman counted the money twice before giving me a receipt for $4,357.

"Harrisong?" she finally said. "Like the family on —"

"Don't I wish," I said, rolling my eyes dramatically.

Of course, she said with her eyes. *What were the chances?*

I watched from the hallway as the agent put the money back in the pencil pouches. I wondered if she noticed the tiny trademarked silhouette of our family on the interior tag.

*   *   *

When we got back to El Rancho, Clara and I stopped at the food court on the mezzanine level to buy milk shakes blended with cookie crumbs. We took them up to the condo and drank them in Clara's bedroom. It almost felt like Normal.

"I hope Dad's feelings won't be hurt when we tell him we took care of the tax thing," Clara said, slurping her frozen concoction through the straw.

"Who's telling Dad anything?" I asked.

She looked at me strangely. "Chums, we *have* to tell Dad."

"No," I said. "Not yet. Dad's terrible with money."

"We paid the IRS back," she said. "The lawyers don't have anything on us now. We can leave. We can go back to Alabama. To the *O'Migosh.*"

154

"No, we can't," I said. "They've got the contract Mom and Dad signed. I read it yesterday."

"What's it say?"

"It's awful," I said, removing a cookie blockage from my straw. "It says Bargain Bonanza owns our right of publicity."

"Our right of *what?*"

I pulled a piece of paper from my pocket. "I copied this from the contract," I began. "'The Right of Publicity prevents the unauthorized commercial use of an individual's name, likeness, or other recognizable aspects of one's persona. It gives an individual the exclusive right to license the use of his or her identity for commercial promotion.'"

"That's what Mom and Dad signed away?" Clara asked.

"Yeah. The contract gives Bargain Bonanza the right to use our names, our pictures, *everything* about us for commercial promotion."

"It's like slavery," she said. "It can't be *legal.*"

"But it is," I said. "It's only illegal if it's unauthorized. By signing the contract, Mom and Dad authorized Bargain Bonanza to do whatever they want with us."

Clara groaned and belched in the same breath. "But the lawyers blackmailed Mom and Dad with the tax thing," she said.

"They'd deny that to a judge."

"Chums, what are you thinking? Tell me."

I told her the rest of the plan. Or started to, anyway.

"SWISS BANK ACCOUNT?!" she yelled. "Are you *nuts?* This isn't a movie."

"Shhhhhh!" I said. "Mom'll hear you. Look, we need money. And we need to be able to hide it somewhere safe."

"We can just keep it here," she said, waving her arms around the room. "In my dresser or closet or somewhere."

"Not safe enough," I said. "Not for the kind of money we need."

"Then we'll use a bank downstairs," she said. "There's one on the mezzanine."

"Clara, I've checked into all this. You've got to fill out paperwork to open an account here. There's a bunch of red tape."

"How much money do we need, anyway?" she said. "Everything's paid for. And now that we've paid that IRS debt —"

"We're not staying here," I said.

"What?"

"We're leaving," I said.

Clara looked at me blankly. Then she put her plastic cup on the dresser. "Chums," she said. "You can't decide this stuff on your own. You have to talk to Mom and —"

"If I tell them, Mom'll just worry. And Dad'll —"

"What?" asked Clara.

"He's so mad," I said. "It's like he's —"

I stopped. But Clara knew what I was thinking.

"He's cracking," she said in a whisper.

"I know," I said.

Clara covered her nose and mouth with her hands. I could see the corners of her mouth were quivering.

"Hey," I said. "It's going to be okay."

She sniffled noisily.

"I've got a plan," I said.

She wiped her nose on her sleeve. Then she grabbed the straw from her cup on the dresser. She stuck the straw in the side of her mouth and began chewing on it, like it was gum.

"Okay, then," she said, smiling. "Tell me how we open a Swiss bank account. But first tell me where in the world you come up with this stuff, Chums."

19.

I had literally stumbled upon it.

A few nights before, when I couldn't sleep, I was lying on my bed, eating a bowl of Cowboy Cal Caramelicious Ice Cream and reading a comic book. I was using my *Economic Theories and Practices* book as a tray for my ice cream. When I finished, I set the bowl on the floor and tossed the book across the room.

The next morning, on my way to the bathroom, I tripped over the economics textbook, which had landed open to page 328. It was a chapter titled "Offshore Banking: The Anonymous Economy." In the middle of the page was a box with the banner "10 Myths about Offshore Banking."

Myth #3: You can't open an offshore account by correspondence.

> *Not true. Most offshore accounts can be opened and maintained by correspondence, using the telephone, Internet, and/or electronic bank transfers.*

Myth #8 also caught my eye.

> *Myth #8: Only criminals use offshore bank accounts.*

> *Not true. Many law-abiding citizens use offshore accounts to conduct business privately and without government interference. Moreover, Swiss bank accounts offer the stability of the Swiss economy, which remains constant even in times of international crisis, thanks to Switzerland's policy of neutrality.*

I remembered what Sophie told me about the founder of Bargain Bonanza. I wondered if that's why he lived in Geneva.

I thought about him. He'd left Bargain Bonanza in the hands of people he trusted. He probably had no idea what had happened to his company.

If we could just find the founder of Bargain Bonanza and tell him what was going on with his company, he'd thank us. He'd let us out of the contract in a heartbeat.

The more I thought about it, the more convinced I became: We had to go to Switzerland. And we had to have money waiting for us there.

*   *   *

For forty-four dollars, I rented a post office box for six months.

"For thirty dollars more, we can get it for a whole year," Clara said, standing in the downtown Dallas post office with me. It was the day after our milk-shake conversation. Clara was wearing a black wig with braids.

"We don't need a year," I said. "We don't even need six months."

But we did need to learn how to drive.

Clara asked several limo drivers to teach us. One driver had the nerve to say he would, but only if Clara would go on a date with him.

"In your dreams," she said.

It was Johnny, the youngest driver in the limo fleet, who finally said he'd give us a driving lesson for fifty dollars. He was probably twenty-two or twenty-three years old.

"This is where my dad taught me," Johnny said as he drove through the iron gates at Oakland Cemetery. "But I didn't learn in a limo. Man, if you can drive this boat, you can drive anything."

Clara caught on right away. I struggled, naturally.

"I really think nine and three seems safer than ten and two," I told Johnny when he said I was putting my hands on the wrong place on the steering wheel.

"You've got it good enough," Clara said from the backseat.

And I did. Good enough.

"You guys planning to go somewhere?" Johnny asked.

"No," I lied. "We just want to learn to drive."

"Okay," he said vaguely.

We told him to leave us in the cemetery, using our usual *We-want-to-walk-home* excuse. The truth was, I needed time to tell Clara the whole plan, beginning with the escape from the condo: how we'd tie up the limo driver, but that we'd leave him a water bottle with a straw so he wouldn't die.

I also needed to tell her how I was researching flight schedules to Geneva, Switzerland, where we would find the founder of Bargain Bonanza, and rental homes in and around the Geneva metro area.

But Clara wanted to look at gravestones first.

"These are so cool," she said, running her hand along the curved outline of an ancient stone marker. "We've gotta get some charcoal and tracing paper next time we're at Bargain BIG-Bonanza."

"Why?" I asked, looking at the sky. Thunder was rumbling in the distance.

"So we can make grave rubbings," she said. "See this angel here? I'd love to do a rubbing of her and hang it in my bedroom. Isn't she cool — in a creepy way?"

"I guess," I said. "Clara?"

"Hmmm?"

"Why do you think you can't write?"

"Huh?"

"The PSAT," I said. "Why were you so upset when you found out there's a creative writing section on the test?"

"Oh," she said, dropping to her knees and pulling a handful of weeds from the base of a grave. "I just don't know how to do that stuff."

"Of course you do," I said. "You're the most creative person I know."

"I'm creative in *some* things," she said. "I wish the PSAT people would let you draw your story instead of write it."

I laughed. "I'm glad they don't. But why do you have a mental block against writing?"

"I don't have a *mental block.* I just don't know how to start a story."

"You can start anywhere you want."

"See, you're not helping," she said. She was speaking to the tombstone. "The way the writing part on the PSAT works is that they give you two or more characters and you have to write a story about them."

"Clara, that's easy."

"For you, it is!" she said, standing up and kicking me in the shins. "I don't know who the characters are or what their story is."

"You just make it up," I said.

"I don't know *how* to make it up," she said through clenched teeth.

"Okay, look," I said. "No matter who the two characters are, you're going to write your PSAT story about a trip they make to a cemetery — this cemetery — at midnight."

"What do they do in the cemetery?"

"How do I know? It's *your* story."

"What if there are a whole bunch of characters?" she asked. "The study guide said they might give you a class of school kids or a family or a basketball team."

"It doesn't matter," I said. "Have them all meet in this cemetery at midnight. Have them meet at this gravestone."

I looked at the weather-beaten stone at my feet.

Leona and Little James

My Wife and Our Angel Baby — Gone but Never Forgotten

Sleep with God, Dear Ones, Until I Join You

"Mother and baby," I said. "She probably died in child-birth, right?"

"That's too sad," Clara said. "I want a happy story."

"Okay, then have your characters meet here at midnight and send them on an adventure somewhere."

"I like that," she said. "If I ever have to make up a story, I'll use that."

"What do you mean *if?*"

"I'm not taking the PSAT," she said. "I just decided."

"Clara," I started. "You *have* to if you want to —"

"No, I don't," she interrupted. "I hate the idea of people I don't know *grading* me on stuff I don't even care about. Maybe I'm not buying into that whole competition thing. Maybe that's not who I am."

She took a breath. "I could get really mad at you right now," she said dramatically.

"At *me?* Why?"

"But I'm not going to," she interrupted, holding up a finger. "Now tell me the plan. I want to know everything."

I began at the end, with our happy life in Switzerland.

"We'll be the Swiss Family Harrisongs," Clara said, and laughed.

I told her how we'd find the founder of Bargain Bonanza in Geneva and ask him to get us out of the contract.

"He totally will, Chums," Clara said simply.

Then I told her about the escape plan — or I started to. But the sky cracked with lightning. Heavy raindrops began pelting us as we ran toward the gates of the cemetery. We sprinted to a bus stop only to realize we didn't have a dime or a cell phone between us. So we ended up running down Malcolm X Boulevard. We ran all the way back to the condo in the drenching rain.

The next morning, the front page of the *Dallas Morning News* had a color photo of Clara and me running in the rain. It was a good picture of Clara. Terrible of me. My eyes were closed, and I was grimacing like an old man.

What bothered me more was that I hadn't seen the photographer. And this was a close-up picture. If someone could see us, that meant someone could also hear us. It meant I had to be very careful where — or if — I told Clara the plan of our escape. There was no room for error. None. I had to get this right.

I'd gotten my family into this mess. I'd get us out of it, too, with or without God's help.

One side has to die, I repeated to myself silently that night as I lay in bed. My job was to figure out how, when, and where.

I already knew who. That part of the plan was easy.

20.

Of course Brandon also had a plan. His was a television series called *The Harrisongs: Live!* It premiered the second Friday night in June. Brandon was executive producer. We watched the first episode in the living room of the condo while we ate Bargain Bonanza Ranchito Burritos.

The show opened with a shot of our family — well, the actors who *played* our family — standing outside a private airport. We're trying to make our way across the tarmac to a small plane, but paparazzi photographers are swarming around us, blocking our entry onto the plane.

"Leave my family alone," Dad's character yells. "Or I'll kill every one of you!"

"Dad, no!" Clara's character wails. She's visibly pregnant now.

"Stand back, Clara," Dad's character commands. "I don't want you or my unborn grandchild to see this."

Dad then pulls a gun from his NormalWear jeans and begins spraying bullets. The cops arrive, throw him in the squad car, and take off in a cloud of smoke while the rest of our family boards the plane in stunned silence.

All this before the first commercial break, which featured back-to-back ads for Bargain Bonanza starring my family — the *real* us.

The Harrisongs: Live! was the first ever Real-vertising show. Or, as *TV Guide* put it, it was the "first seamless integration of reality-driven drama and advertising" in the history of television. I learned more about Real-vertising from *TV Guide* than I ever did in those Brand Identity meetings. This is from the issue of *TV Guide* that had a picture of our family on the cover, alongside the actors who portrayed us:

> **Designed to appeal to a more sophisticated television audience, Real-vertising combines the drama of reality TV with the skill of professional actors, who, in the case of *The Harrisongs: Live!*, are better able to portray the beautiful and maddening complexities of a *real* family.**
>
> **The actual Harrisongs appear in commercials scattered tastefully throughout *The Harrisongs: Live!* But the bigger advertising punch is packed within the**

show itself, where characters are shown wearing and using *only* Bargain Bonanza NormalWear products, just as the *real* Harrisongs presumably do in real life.

The Friday night show is shot and edited just one day before it airs, making it clean, fresh, and "better than live," says executive producer Brandon Greidov.

After the first episode, I heard Dad in the kitchen, talking into his Bargain Bonanza cell phone.

"You can't do this," he said. "I won't allow it. (Pause.) It's me. Frank. Harrisong."

Oh, brother.

"I don't care what we signed," Dad continued. "I'm *un*signing it now. (Pause.) The *what?* What kind of input? Does that mean you'll listen to us? Well. Maybe. All right. Okay. Good-bye, Brandon."

And that's how my family became creative consultants to the television show allegedly based on us.

* * *

"The writers come in on Monday mornings," explained Brandon when we arrived at our first *The Harrisongs: Live!* production meeting at Bargain Bonanza TV studios. "They review all the tapes and material from the weekend."

"Material from the weekend?" Mom asked.

"You know, the stuff you guys do all weekend," Brandon said. "Mall openings. Catalog shoots. Going to church and shopping. This is *your* show. We use stuff from your real lives."

"The hell you do," Dad said. "I've never pulled a gun on anybody in my life."

"Oh," Brandon said. "That. Well, we have to jazz things up a little. Sometimes life isn't all that exciting, right?"

"Why do I have to be a raving lunatic?" Dad asked. "And why does Clara have to be pregnant? Or Ben a dumbcluck? The whole thing's ridiculous."

"Because it's *dramatic*," Brandon said. "This is a television show, for God's sake. And, Frank, you're obviously dealing with some hostility issues and —"

"And because Bargain Bonanza is introducing a new line of *Frankly Protection* devices, otherwise known as handguns. And isn't there a new line of teen maternity wear, Brandon? Hi, I'm Sam, lead writer for your show."

He looked like a kid in his worn jeans and navy blazer.

"Hi," every member of my family said in unison, like a pack of trained seals.

Sam laughed. Then he shook hands with Mom and Dad.

"This must be weird for you," Sam said. "To have a hit show based on your family."

"It's a hit show?" said Dad.

"Yeah," said Sam. "Didn't they tell you? We were the highest-rated show on Friday night. Sales of Bargain Bonanza are —" He looked to Brandon for help.

"You know this stuff better than I do," Sam said. "What're the numbers?"

Brandon's brow furrowed.

"I'm not sure," he said. "They're fifteen or twenty percent up."

"After just one show," Sam said, turning to us with a laugh. "Do you guys know how *amazing* that is? Basically, your show is an hour-long commercial for Bargain Bonanza. My writing team and I have to craft story lines that involve every product category. Do you know how hard it is to work Cowboy Cal One-Mix Campfire DinnerFix into a —"

"It's reality-driven TV with aggressive product placement," snapped Brandon. "It's Real-vertising. Perhaps you've heard of it, Sam."

Sam laughed. "I was only trying to explain what the series was."

"The series doesn't *need* your explanations," Brandon said. "We just need a new script for the third episode."

"It's done," Sam said. "I e-mailed it to you."

"I know," Brandon said. "And I rejected it. I want a rewrite."

"But I thought —"

"It wasn't credible," said Brandon. "It wasn't real."

"Well, it's not *real,*" Sam said. Again, he was laughing, but now it was a high-pitched, nervous laugh.

Brandon started to walk away.

"I'll have a rewrite to you by tomorrow afternoon," Sam yelled after him.

"Don't bother," said Brandon, turning around: "I'm writing it myself."

Sam tried to laugh, but he started choking.

"He's kidding," Sam said to us, recovering his breath. "I think."

And then, almost as an afterthought, Sam said: "You know, Brandon gets a percentage of NormalWear profits. Lucky dog."

21.

We returned to the soundstage on Wednesday for the read-through of episode two of *The Harrisongs: Live!*

"Everybody, these are the Harrisongs," Brandon said, gesturing toward us with a dismissive wave of his hand. "If you have any questions about your character, you can ask them. But not until after we finish the read-through."

The actors began assembling around a long table covered with trays of fruit and bottled water. The girl who played Clara was a sickly-looking waif. She wore a silk kimono with a muslin feedbag slung around her neck.

"I'm trying to get used to being pregnant," she told the group.

"Same here," Clara whispered to me.

The actors who portrayed Mom and Dad were laughing uproariously about something. It struck me as odd because

I'd rarely seen my *real* mom and dad laugh so recklessly or act so physically playful with each other.

Laura's counterpart sat with her agent, a wiry woman who was underlining the young actress's lines with a yellow highlighter.

"This was *supposed* to be a supporting actress role," the woman complained. "I just don't see it here."

There were two Sallys. Federal law forbids infants from working more than a few hours a day. So a pair of six-month-old twins, Lindsey and Brittney, played Sally, who immediately forgot she was mad at being portrayed as an infant. Sally fell in love with the babies and petted them timidly with a stiffened hand, just like she used to pet her beloved rabbits.

Ben sulked in the hallway. He didn't want to meet Ned, the young actor who played him. Ned was an odd-looking boy with an unusually large head. But, to the kid's credit, he approached Ben in the hallway and introduced himself.

"I'm not really retarded, you know," Ned said.

"Me neither!" said Ben, delighted.

An hour later I heard Ben ask Mom if Ned could come to the condo sometime for a sleepover.

The kid who played me was a young actor named Seth. He wore owlish glasses and had carefully tousled black hair, not unlike the illustration of Harry Potter on the cover of those popular books. Seth showed zero interest in meeting me.

I didn't care. I had more important things to think about than a stupid TV show. I spent that Wednesday making a mental list of things I needed to get: printer cartridges, watches, jewelry. These were the smallest and easiest things to sell to pawn shops, which is exactly what I did the next day.

* * *

"I've got a really bad headache," I told Mom.

We were standing in the kitchen. She was watching her morning coffee drip through the Bargain Bonanza coffeemaker.

"Do you mind if I don't go to the set today?" I asked.

"Okay," Mom said distractedly. "Take some aspirin, honey."

As soon as she and the others left, I dialed *7. When the limo driver arrived, I asked him to take me to the newest Bargain Bonanza Extravaganza.

"I'll find another way home," I said when he dropped me off.

As I walked back to the condo, I stopped at three pawn shops and converted the Bargain Bonanza loot to cash. I then proceeded to a bank two blocks from the condo, where I exchanged the cash for a money order, which I sent by overnight mail to my newly opened Swiss bank account.

Clara still didn't understand the reason for this.

"We need money," I explained to her that night. We were talking in her bedroom. "Because we're going to have to lie low for a while."

"We're going to be on the *lam*," Clara said, making snaky arm moves.

"Clara, this is *serious*. We're going to need money to live on until we find him."

"*Who?*" she said.

"The founder of Bargain Bonanza," I said, exasperated.

"Oh, right," she said. "I forgot. So tell me the rest of the plan."

I started to tell her, beginning from where we tie up the limo driver. But the doorbell rang.

It was a courier from *The Harrisongs: Live!* production department. He had a large envelope for us. I opened it and immediately recognized Sophie's handwriting.

You're all booked to fly to London tomorrow (Friday). Here are your passports. Ben, if you've lost yours, let me know. Interviews are scheduled this weekend. Photo shoot for HELLO! on Monday. BBC interview on Tuesday. Madame Tussauds on Wednesday morning. Wednesday afternoon is free. Iris will accompany you to handle media and logistics. — Sophie

The sight of her handwriting made me queasy. To think how once I would've kept the note and studied it, looking for secret messages to me hidden within it. Now I saw only how she'd pawned us off on Iris in Asia.

Oh well. I was thankful that she — or someone — had gotten us passports. I'd forgotten about that. We'd need passports to get to Switzerland.

I didn't see the second episode of *The Harrisongs: Live!* because we were flying to London and our crummy Bargain Bonanza TV/DVD programmer/recorder didn't work.

(Big surprise there. And that was another thing I couldn't wait to discuss with the founder of Bargain Bonanza when we met him in Switzerland. He'd be *furious* when he heard how junky everything in his stores was.)

Ben enjoyed playing tour guide in London. "So they've got this queen, see, and she lives in a castle," he told Laura and Sally on the limo ride from Heathrow Airport.

"A *real* castle?" Sally asked.

"Of course a real castle," Ben said. "With dragons and everything. Last time I was here, they let me go inside and pet the dragons. Usually the dragons bite people, but they liked me because —"

"Ben," Mom said. "Enough."

We stayed at The Ritz-Carlton. Mom wanted to have tea at Harrods department store, but we got mobbed at the front entrance.

"The show's on here, too?" Dad asked Iris.

"Of course!" Iris chirped. "It's on everywhere, except Latin America. That's the only market you're not in yet. We're still negotiating licensing fees for NormalWear there. But they love you here — and everywhere. You're huge in Hong Kong."

We spent the weekend doing interviews. This is when the TV host asked me when I knew our family had become a household name.

Other questions were even worse: *Do you love being famous? What's the best thing about being a star? Clara, can I have your autograph? It's for my son. He's in love with you.*

The BBC interview went pretty much like the others: *Are you surprised by the phenomenal success of your show? What's your daily schedule like?*

Laura and Sally giggled at the British pronunciation of *schedule* as *shed-jewel.*

"That's how people talk over here," Ben told them. Then, to the BBC host: "I'm the only one in my family who's ever been to England before."

The interview ended with the host asking us: "Before you leave, tell us about the big surprise planned for the third episode."

She was holding a tabloid magazine with our picture on the cover under the words: "Can It Be True? SHOCKING Revelation on the Next Episode of *The Harrisongs: Live!*"

"No idea," said Dad, folding his arms across his chest. "Interesting, isn't it? Considering the show's supposed to be about us."

"Oh, please," the interviewer begged. "Just a tiny clue?"

"We really haven't the faintest idea," Mom said.

On Wednesday morning, we had to pose for two hours at Madame Tussauds wax museum.

"Next time you come to London, you'll be able to see yourself — in wax!" Iris said as the wax artist took countless photos and measurements of us.

We spent that afternoon wandering around London. Mom insisted we see the Magna Carta and St. Paul's Cathedral.

"Why do we have to do *school* stuff here?" Laura whined.

"Because your education is important," Mom said. "You have to know history and math and —"

"No, you don't," Laura interrupted. "All you need to know is how to give a good sound bite."

"And how to look cute on TV," Sally added.

I watched Mom's jaw clench. So much for home-schooling.

As we were leaving St. Paul's, Dad asked Iris what the BBC interviewer meant about the big surprise planned for episode three.

"Who knows?" Iris shrugged. "Brandon's writing and editing the whole thing. I can't wait to see it!"

We left the next morning. Before our flight, Iris took the little kids to the airport gift shop to buy reading material for the long trip. Laura got fashion magazines. Sally chose *The Big Book of Fun Facts & Trivia*. Ben was thrilled to find a "classic" edition of *Pirate Tales to Tremble By*.

"This was the best part of the trip," Ben told Mom as he plopped next to her in a padded chair in the first-class lounge. "From now on, can I study the history of pirates 'stead of that *Magnum* Carta stuff?"

Mom didn't respond.

"Mom," said Ben, waving the pirate book in front of her face. "I'm just going to study pirate stuff from now on, 'kay?"

"Okay," Mom sighed.

That's when I knew she'd given up.

On the flight to Dallas, I sat across the aisle from a woman reading a tabloid with our picture on the cover under the words "Big Shocker This Week!"

"I can't *wait* to see what happens on tomorrow night's show," she gushed.

"Me neither," I said.

Clara had the window seat next to me. I watched her paint clouds using a candy bar–sized set of watercolor paints she'd bought at Marks & Spencer.

I thought about telling her the rest of the plan, but I didn't. I couldn't. Too many people sitting around us. I had to be careful.

But the truth was, I was too afraid to say the plan out loud. Our lives were at stake — and, of course, other people's lives, too. I had to get this right.

I pretended to sleep on the flight to Dallas, but I really spent those hours praying silently:

Dear God, for once in my life, will You let things work how I want them to work? Please? I know what I'm doing. Let my plan work. Please. Thank You. Amen.

22.

When we returned to the condo on Thursday night, we found a note from Richard, slipped under the door.

"They gave us a bonus," Dad said, throwing a fistful of Bargain Bonanza Buckeroos on the kitchen counter. "Whoopee."

Richard's note said we should relax for a while. "Shake off the jet lag," he wrote. No interviews or appearances were scheduled for the next two weeks.

On Friday morning, I tried to slip out of the condo unnoticed. But Mom saw me dialing *7 and asked where I was going.

"I want to check out that new Bargain Bonanza SuperFantastic Store near the Galleria," I said.

"Why in the world would you want to do that?" she asked.

"Something to do," I shrugged.

"Sally'n'me want to go, too," Laura said. "We need roller skates."

The in-line skaters blasting around Piccadilly Circus in London had reminded Laura of her love of roller-skating. She said the hallway outside our condo was the perfect place to skate.

"And it'd be safer than the sidewalk 'cause there are no cars," Laura said.

But I didn't want my little sisters tagging along on my last ever shopping trip to Bargain Bonanza.

"Can I please just go alone?" I begged Mom. "I need some . . . personal stuff."

"Like what?" she pressed.

"Mom," I said, trying to look anguished.

She retreated immediately. My puberty ploy always worked with her.

"Maybe you could bring back a treat for the girls," Mom suggested as I was leaving.

The newest Bargain Bonanza SuperFantastic Store was twenty minutes away. I asked Johnny the limo driver to wait for me outside. I knew it wouldn't take long to buy a hundred DVDs with my stack of Bargain Bonanza Buckeroos.

On the way back, I suggested to Johnny that we stop at Slippy's Ice Cream Shack. It was next to my favorite pawn shop, and I knew Johnny's girlfriend worked at Slippy's. While he flirted with her, I converted my DVDs to cash next door.

I didn't remember the treat I was supposed to pick up for Laura and Sally until I was leaving the pawn shop and saw a pile of used in-line skates by the door. I dug through the skates and found two pairs that looked about Laura's and Sally's sizes. I paid the pawn shop owner twenty dollars from the stack of bills he'd just given me. He stuffed the skates in a blue plastic Bargain Bonanza bag. That's when it hit him.

"Bargain Bonanza," the owner said as I was leaving. "*That's* where I've seen you. You're the kid who does those funny ads for Cowboy Chaz Gotta Go laxatives."

I left without answering.

When I got home, Mom and Dad were in the kitchen. Mom was taking a Bargain Bonanza frozen *Pizz-Ah!* out of the oven.

"What's this big surprise everyone's talking about?" Dad asked. "Even the concierge asked me what was going to happen to us on tonight's show."

"Will you just *forget* about it?" Mom said wearily. "Anyone with half a brain knows it's not us."

"We don't have to watch it," Dad said. "I'm not going to."

After dinner, Dad tightened and greased the wheels on Sally's and Laura's skates.

"Look at this crap Bargain Bonanza's selling," he said. "These skates are *used*."

When the theme song for *The Harrisongs: Live!* started playing on the TV in the living room, Dad grabbed a broom and left. I could hear him in the hallway.

"What's he doing?" I asked.

"Sweeping, I guess," Mom said. She sounded so tired. So defeated.

"It's starting!" Laura yelled. She was unabashedly enthralled by the show — mainly because her TV character was sassy and mischievous, which she liked.

"Mom, can we have our dessert in the living room?" Ben asked.

"If you're careful," Mom said.

Ben and Laura grabbed their cereal bowls of ice cream and ran to the sofa. Sally stretched out on the floor, her head propped up by one pawlike hand as she shoveled ice cream in her mouth with the other. Clara and I sat cross-legged on the floor with our bowls in front of us.

The third episode of *The Harrisongs: Live!* was as ridiculous as the first. It began with our preparations for the England trip. We're taught how to curtsy and bow. Then we arrive in London, where we're compared to the Beatles ("They may not be the Fab Four, but they're the Sensational Seven!"). Mom and Dad take Ben to see a specialist in the hopes that she can cure him. The rest of us sneak off to have high tea with the queen, who scolds Clara for her "situation." Clara, depressed, visits a church alone: a nice opportunity to show off Bargain Bonanza's new It's Normal to be Spiritual line of incense, candles, and chalices. And then, on the flight home, Ben has a seizure.

"I hate being retarded," Ben said gruffly, slumping out of the living room with his empty ice-cream bowl.

"You're not *really* retarded," Sally yelled after him. "It's just a TV show."

A silly, stupid, nonsensical TV show. And, on top of everything else, it was boring. This was the best Brandon could do?

I thought the episode was over when I saw Sally (the real Sally) skip across the screen in a commercial for Bargain Bonanza Sneakin' Sneakers. I stood up to take my ice-cream bowl to the kitchen, but stopped when I saw there was one more scene in the show.

Clara's character and mine were sitting in her bedroom, drinking cans of Bargain Bonanza Cowboy Cal Cola.

"I'm worried about Dad," my character said. "He's terrible with money."

"I know," Clara's character said. "And lately it's like he's cracking."

I froze.

"SWISS BANK ACCOUNT!?" Clara's character said. "Chubs, what're you saying?"

Laura howled on the couch. "Charles, she called you 'Chubs'!"

"I'm saying we have to leave," my character said on TV.

Clara and I were now both standing inches away from the television screen.

"Move!" Sally yelled behind us. "I can't see what's happening."

"I'll go," Clara's character was saying solemnly. "But I'm not giving up my baby."

"Mom and Dad think you should give the baby up for adoption," my character replied.

"This is *my* child," Clara's character said piously. "I'm not leaving without my baby. Now tell me the plan again, starting from when we call for the limo."

It was too impossible to believe. The production credits were rolling over the image of Clara and me sitting on her bed. She was rubbing her swollen belly and smiling tenderly.

Clara looked at me. "Oh my God. They're —"

Dad walked in the front door.

"The skating rink is now officially open for business," he said grandly as he returned the broom to the hall closet.

"Yay!" Laura and Sally squealed. They bolted from the living room.

Clara and I stood in stunned silence as the promo for next week's show played: *"Tune in next Friday night when we'll see the Harrisongs begin to crack under the pressure. Was the price of fame too high?"*

"I can't wait to see what happens next week," Laura sang as she and Sally strapped on their skates.

"Me neither," said Sally, wobbling in her skates to the door. She punched the security code into the door panel and pulled the knob.

"Hey, I can't open the door," Sally said.

"Let me do it," Laura said. She used her index finger to tap out the code. Then she pulled on the door. "The door's stuck," she said, pulling again unsuccessfully.

"No, it's not," Dad said. "I was just out there a minute ago."

Dad entered the security code into the panel. "What the heck?" he said, turning the knob. The door refused to open.

He punched in the security code again, slowly. Nothing.

"Maybe it's an electrical thing," Mom said, picking up the phone. "Strange that the lights are still on. I'll just call —"

I knew from the expression on her face that the line was dead.

"I'll call downstairs," Dad said, pulling his Bargain Bonanza cell phone out of the charger that sat on the kitchen counter. "They'll send someone up from maintenance. This is what cell phones are for."

But of course service had been cut off to all of our cell phones.

"This is just like what Edward Teach did," Ben said. He still had *Pizz-Ah!* sauce on his chin.

"Who?" Mom said.

"Edward Teach," Ben repeated. "The famous pirate. He took over a cargo ship sailing out of Charleston, South Carolina. There were people and little kids onboard. He took them all prisoner and locked them in the hold of the ship and said he was going to hang them if —"

"Stop that!" Mom said.

But it was too late. Sally was already crying.

"Nobody's taken us hostage," Dad said.

But in a sense, somebody had. Because there we were, locked in, cut off, and stranded in a penthouse condo in downtown Dallas.

23.

Mom ordered Ben, Laura, and Sally to their bedrooms.

"What's happening?" Laura asked.

"Nothing," Mom said breathlessly. "Go to bed. We'll have everything sorted out by morning."

"But what'll we *eat?*" Laura asked. "If we're locked in here forever, what'll we —"

"We're not locked in," Mom said. "There's just a problem with the door. Now go to sleep."

"Can we roller-skate tomorrow?" Sally asked.

"Yes," Mom said, pushing Sally and Laura down the hall.

"*I'm* not going to bed now," Ben said. "It's nine o'clock at night."

"Take your pirate book in your room and read," Mom said.

"But —"

"*Now!*"

I pulled Clara in the front hall closet and closed the door behind us. A blanket fell on my head.

"They've got cameras in here," I whispered.

"In my bedroom," Clara said. "That means they know —"

"They don't know everything," I whispered.

"How do you know?" she said. "Ow. You're standing on my foot."

I moved.

"We never talked about going to Geneva when we were in your room," I said. "Just about the bank account."

"You're right," she said. "We talked about Switzerland in the cemetery. So unless Brandon implanted cameras in our bodies or something, he doesn't know the whole plan."

Clara, you don't even know the whole plan, I thought.

"Dad could find the cameras and turn them so they're facing the wall," Clara said.

"But then Brandon would know we know," I said. "We can't do that."

"I don't want people *watching* me in my bedroom. They can see me changing my clothes. It's disgusting."

We crouched in silence.

"Dad could find where the cameras are and make a map

of the condo," I said. "There've gotta be places the cameras can't see."

"Like the bathrooms," Clara said. She covered her face with both hands. "If they've been watching me go to the bathroom, I'll die."

"Don't worry," I said. "They'll be sorry."

"Chums —"

"I have a plan."

"Okay, so how do we get out?" she asked.

"I don't know yet," I said. "But I know one thing."

"What?"

"We've got to produce the next episode of *The Harrisongs: Live!*"

"*What?*" Clara yelled.

"Shhhhhh," I whispered, covering her mouth. "I'll write the script. Dad'll find a safe place for us to practice. Mom can teach the little kids their lines."

"What do I do?" she asked.

I thought for a minute. *What could Clara do?*

"You've got to take care of your baby," I said.

She pushed me. "Quit it, *Chubs.*"

But I could see she was smiling. And then we both started laughing. It was the completely inappropriate laughter of two people who know their next decisions will determine the rest of their lives.

"You can write letters to the newspaper and TV stations," I said. "We'll mail the letters as we're leaving."

"And say *what?*"

"We want the media to force Brandon to broadcast the video from our last days here," I said.

"Chums, I don't want people seeing a video of me — "

"We're going to be acting," I said. "I'm going to write our lines for us."

"And I've got to write letters?" she said. "You know I don't like writing."

"Okay, I'll do that part. You be in charge of the passports."

"Just finding all our passports? I think they're in Mom's —"

"No," I said. "You've got to change them. We'll need new identities in Switzerland. Make us the Harrisons or the Harrises or the Hares."

"*Harrisons* will be easiest," Clara said. "People spell it like that all the time. Should I change our first names, too?"

"No," I said. "Yeah. I don't care. Just as long as they're believable."

We heard a loud bang followed by the sound of Dad yelling: "It's a damn *fire* hazard is what it is!"

Clara winced. "We've got to tell Mom and Dad," she said. "I'll tell Dad. You tell Mom."

When we opened the closet door, we found Dad trying to break the front doorjamb with his shoe. Mom was in the kitchen, still fiddling with the phones.

"I need to show you something in my room," I told Mom.

Clara led Dad to the front hall closet and pushed him in.

Our acting careers began the next morning.

24.

"As long as we're stuck inside, we might as well get some housecleaning done," Mom said the next morning. "Ben, dear, why don't you help Daddy wash all the light fixtures? The rest of you can help me with the bedrooms and closets. This will be fun, children!"

Ugh, Mom. Stop overacting.

But she couldn't help it. The previous night when I'd pulled her under my bed and told her about the hidden cameras in the condo, she didn't believe me.

"It's just a television show," she'd said, squinting till her eyes adjusted to the darkness below my bed. "Everyone has to remember that it's *not* our family. It's not about us."

"But that last scene of Clara and me in her bedroom," I explained. "Talking about how Dad was cracking? That was *real*."

When I finally convinced Mom, her breathing became

shallow and labored. She gripped my hand and said an Our Father with her eyes closed. I worried she might start to cry — or want to say a rosary together. So I quickly told her how Clara and I had settled up with the IRS, and how I'd opened a Swiss bank account.

"*$32,800!?*" Mom gasped, when I told her how much I'd deposited in the account.

"Shhhhhh!" I said. But I couldn't help laughing.

As I explained how Clara and I had converted the Bargain Bonanza Buckeroos to cash, Mom's eyes grew bright.

"Don't tell the little kids about the cameras," she whispered.

"We have to."

"Not yet," she said. "I don't want to scare the girls. And who knows what Ben'll do. We'll wait till the last minute to tell them."

Hence, Mom's overacting the next morning.

"*Housecleaning?*" Sally whined. "But you said we could go roller-skating today."

"Darling," Mom began brightly.

"Let 'em skate," Dad said. "That's even better."

He was right. Laura and Sally's Roller Derby antics in the kitchen provided the perfect distraction for the task at hand.

Dad attacked his job with gusto, standing on furniture

and aimlessly dusting the ceiling with an old T-shirt while he searched for hidden cameras. I asked him to check my bedroom first. He found only one tiny camera lens, the size of a postage stamp. It was focused on my writing desk.

So I wrote the script under my bed with a flashlight. From there, I could hear Ben's muffled voice, complaining bitterly about having to work while "everyone else in the *whole world* gets to goof off."

At noon, Clara crawled under my bed with two peanut-butter sandwiches wrapped in a paper towel. She handed one to me.

"Thanks," I whispered. I set aside the script, which I'd titled simply *Episode 4*.

"Dad's done your room, the living room, and the kitchen," Clara said quietly.

"Is he finding cameras?" I asked.

"Yeah. He's going to tell us where they are tonight so we can avoid them."

"Okay, good," I said. "What's everyone else doing?"

"Mom's fixing lunch for Sally and Laura. Ben's practicing."

"Practicing?" I said, taking a bite of the sandwich. "What's he practicing?"

"Chopping people's heads off with a sword," she said. "You know, his pirate thing."

"He's twelve," I said. "Sometimes I think he's really retarded."

"Be nice, Chums. Ben's just being Ben. How's the script coming?"

"Okay," I said. "Today's Saturday, right?"

"Right," Clara said, chewing her sandwich.

"I'll have it finished on Monday."

"Then what?"

"I'll need to make copies," I said, forgetting for a moment that we were locked in and had no access to a photocopier. "Can you help me copy the script by hand?"

"Sure," she said, licking peanut butter off her knuckle. "We can do that on Tuesday. Then what?"

"We have to practice," I said.

"Wednesday is read-through," Clara said, imitating Brandon's voice. "This will be hard for Laura and Sally. And even Ben."

"I didn't give them many lines," I said. "It's Mom and Dad I'm worried about."

"Why?"

"They can't act," I hissed. "Did you hear Mom this

morning? *'Won't this be lovely, my darlings?'* Dad's not much better. It's driving me crazy."

Clara laughed. "They'll do fine."

"I hope so," I said.

I looked at Clara. She always looked so different in the dark.

"You okay?" I asked.

"Yeah," she said. "It's just that —"

"What?"

"You think we're doing the right thing?" she asked.

"Of course we are," I said. "You don't want to live like this forever, do you?"

"No," she said. "But I'm just wondering —"

"What?"

"That stuff you said about somebody having to die," she said. "The thing that philosopher said."

"Hegel," I reminded her. "He said the only way a conflict between right and right can end is with the death of one side or the other."

"Do you think that's true?"

"I know it is," I said, turning back to my script. "Let me finish this, okay? I'm almost done."

"Okay," she said, scooting out from under the bed. "But I told you you'd write again."

25.

On Wednesday morning, we had a family meeting in the master bathroom off Mom and Dad's bedroom. (Much to Clara's relief, Dad said there were *no* cameras in any of the bathrooms.)

Mom and Dad took turns explaining the plan to Ben, Laura, and Sally: how it was almost time for us to leave Dallas; how Dad was going to break the front door so we could get out; how we wouldn't be able to take much with us.

"This is just like when we left Normal — only sneakier," Laura said. She was sitting in the sink and fiddling with the hot water faucet.

"It's better," Ben said darkly. "Man, this is going to be like a *mutiny*."

"This isn't a game," Mom said in a whisper. "Or a joke. We have to do this right. Everyone has to pay attention."

"Where're we gonna go after we escape?" Ben asked. "I vote for South America."

"One thing at a time," Dad said. He was sitting on the closed toilet. "We've got to do this little play first."

Clara passed out the scripts. She'd highlighted everyone's parts for them.

"I don't get it," Sally said. "It's *lying*, isn't it?"

"It's acting," Mom said. "Sometimes it's okay to make things up."

As we rehearsed in the bathroom, Mom continued to overplay every line.

"Maybe you could just say it like you'd normally say it," Dad suggested. "Pretend like you're not acting."

"Okay," Mom said. "Let me start again from the top of page four." She cleared her voice. "I cannot and I will not —"

"Robot reading," Sally said. She was stretched out in the Jacuzzi tub.

"*What?*" said Mom.

"You're robot reading," Sally said. "That's what our teacher used to call it when someone in our class read like a robot. I. Can. Not. And. I. Will. Not."

"I'm doing the best I can," Mom said.

"She's doing fine," Clara said. "Everybody just be quiet so we can get through this. Mom, start again. Page four."

It took us almost three hours to read through the twenty-two-page script. We had to take frequent breaks to walk through the condo. I wanted to prove to whoever was monitoring the cameras that we were still there. We hadn't left yet.

"I love being a *real* actress!" Laura sang in the front hallway during one of our breaks.

I pulled her in the front hall closet and told her to cool it.

"We won't be ready by tomorrow," Mom whispered to me when we stopped for lunch. "We need another day to practice."

"Can't," I whispered. I was squatting in front of the stove, out of view of the hidden camera Dad had found on top of the kitchen cupboards.

Mom crouched beside me. "Why not?"

"We have to do it Thursday night," I said softly. "Brandon shoots the show and edits all night Thursday. He won't have time to watch us — the *real* us. We'll mail letters to the newspapers and TV stations on our way to the airport. The media will force Brandon to show our tape on Friday night, in place of his show. By then, we'll be in Geneva, Switzerland."

"But they can track us," Mom said. "Our passports —"

"We're *changing* our passports," I said. "Clara's working on that."

"What about plane tickets?"

"I've got money," I said, standing. "We'll pay cash at the airport."

Just let me do this, I felt like saying. *Everybody do what I say. I'm the director. I'm the producer. I have a plan.*

* * *

Of course nobody stayed on script. Especially not Ben.

"Hey, look," he said, pulling something furry out of a box. "I found a dead mouse in here. This is the *ninth* mouse I've found in a box of Cowboy Cal One-Mix Campfire DinnerFix."

We were sitting around the kitchen table on Thursday night. Mom looked to me to steer the conversation back to the script.

"I guess what I'll remember most are the lies," I said. "The way Brandon and Richard and Sophie Buchanan and everyone else lied to us."

"About everything," said Dad. "From the very first day we met them, they —"

"Hey, Mom," Laura interrupted. "If Ben found a dead mouse in nine out of every ten boxes of Cowboy Cal One-Mix Campfire DinnerFix, that'd be ninety percent, right?"

Mom left the table, laughing. When she returned, I scratched my nose. Her cue.

"Oh," she said. "Right. So. Why don't we go around the table and say the thing we hate most about Bargain Bonanza. Whoops. I mean, let's all say the thing we won't *miss* the most. I'll start. What I really won't miss about Bargain Bonanza are the tasteless and un-, er, I mean *non*-nutritious meals."

She used a dramatic hand gesture to take in all the Bargain Bonanza canned goods and boxed meals we'd piled on the table.

"Back in Normal, Illinois, this is exactly the kind of food I *didn't* feed my family," Mom continued.

She turned and stared at Dad.

"What?" he said. "Oh, yeah. Well, let me just say this: Bargain Bonanza's tools are cheap, poorly made, and dangerous. That's what you get when you use plastic. Frankly, I think they're worthless crap."

Laura and Clara talked about how much they didn't like NormalWear clothes. Ben was supposed to say he thought Little Benny watches made telling time hard. Instead, he ad-libbed.

"Do you think it's true that they put cockroach turds in Bargain Bonanza Oh-Boy Beefitos?" he asked earnestly.

"Ben," Sally said. "It's my turn. And I just want to say I *hate* Cowboy Cal Kooky Cookies. Right, Charles?"

Someone was pounding at our door.

"Open up!" a voice in the hall shouted.

"Wow," Clara whispered, looking at me. "That was fast."

Dad marched to the door. The rest of us followed.

"We can't open the door, remember?" Dad said, winking at me. "We're locked in here. You should know that. Brandon, is that you?"

"If you don't open this door, we'll be forced to break it down," the voice said.

"Go ahead!" Dad laughed. "You'll save me the job." He pushed us into the living room. "Cover your eyes."

"We're coming in," the voices said. There was more than one person in the hall. They were using a megaphone.

"Be our guest!" Dad yelled.

The door came crashing down. Three men in uniforms climbed over it.

"Dallas Police Department," the tallest officer said.

"And Texas Department of Family and Protective Services," said a woman with short gray hair standing in the hallway.

"*What?*" Mom asked. "What is this?"

"We're taking Clara and Laura Harrisong into protective custody," the officer said.

"Clara and Laura aren't going anywhere without us," Dad snarled.

"You're coming, too," the officer said. "All of you. To police headquarters for questioning."

26.

Sirens screamed as we sped through downtown Dallas. My family was separated in two police cars: Clara and Laura in one, the rest of us crowded in another.

"I've never been in a real *pleeece* car," Sally informed the officer in the front seat.

When we arrived at the police station, Mom, Dad, Ben, Sally, and I were escorted by armed officers into a windowless room that smelled like disinfectant.

"You're a real *cop,* aren't you?" Ben asked the weasly looking officer assigned to guard us. "Not just a Bargain Bonanza security guard, right?"

The officer nodded without smiling.

"Where are Laura and Clara?" Dad demanded.

"They're being examined," the officer said flatly. "A doctor will examine all the children."

"We hafta go to a *doctor?*" Sally asked. "Why do we hafta —"

"It's okay, honey," Mom said. Her eyes were bleary with tears. She turned to the officer: "This joke has gone too far."

"This ain't no joke, ma'am," the officer said.

Mom flinched at the word *ain't.*

A woman cop with a potbelly arrived to take Sally and Ben to the examining room.

"You can stay here for the moment," the cop said, pointing at me. "Lieutenant Wilson needs to ask you and your parents some questions."

Dad paced. Mom and I sat in silence on the hard plastic chairs. I could feel the vibration of her short, shallow breathing through the connected chairs.

Minutes later, Lieutenant Wilson walked in the room and closed the door behind him. He had thick, dark eyebrows that formed an awning over his eyes. He pulled a chair to the center of the room and sat on it.

"I don't think I need to tell you why you're here," he began.

"You damn well *do* need to tell us," Dad snarled. "If this is something those lawyers dreamed up to —"

Lieutenant Wilson interrupted. "Your hostility has been

a problem in the past, Harrisong. If I have to put you in lockup, I will."

Dad sat down next to Mom.

"Just tell us what this is all about," Mom said. "Please."

"We've received videotapes," Lieutenant Wilson said.

Oh, thank God. It was just that.

"We can explain," said Dad.

"Really?" Lieutenant Wilson said. "I'd like to hear how you explain the scene of you and your teenage daughter emerging from a front hall closet."

What?

"We also have videotape of Clara leaving the same closet with her brother," Lieutenant Wilson continued, looking at me. "And a video of Charles and Laura leaving the same closet."

He put his paperwork on his lap and glared at Dad and me.

"I don't know what's going on with your family," he said. "But this doesn't look good."

"What are you saying?" Mom asked.

"I'm saying that we have enough evidence to charge your husband right now, and to call the juvenile detention office to report Charles."

What?

"We were . . . I was . . . Clara and I were just talking," I stammered. "And I only took Laura in the closet to tell her to be —"

"But instead," Lieutenant Wilson continued, ignoring me, "because I don't know where the tapes came from, I'm going to remove Laura and Clara from the home. Until we get a clearer picture of the situation that's —"

Dad stood up and took a step forward. "How dare you even —"

"Frank, stop!" Mom said. She turned to Lieutenant Wilson. "You don't think —"

"It's not just what I *think*," Wilson replied. "It's also what the girls said. They're scared of the situation in your home. Clara told the officers that on the drive down here."

"You're making this up," Dad said. "I don't believe you."

Lieutenant Wilson left the room to make a phone call. When he returned, he told us to follow him through a maze of hallways. We passed examining rooms, break rooms, reception desks, and a line of derelicts in handcuffs until we reached Room 147-B.

It was a fiercely lit green room with a vinyl couch, two plastic chairs, and a coffee table filled with dog-eared hunting magazines. Clara and Laura were sitting on the couch.

"Honey," Mom said, hugging both girls at once.

"Where are Ben and Sally?" Dad asked.

"They'll be joining us shortly," Lieutenant Wilson said.

I tried to make eye contact with Clara, but she wouldn't look at me.

"Do you want to tell them what you told us?" Lieutenant Wilson asked Clara. A beat of silence. "Or should I?"

Clara didn't answer. She didn't even look up.

"What the girls told us," Lieutenant Wilson said, speaking unnaturally slowly, "is that they're frightened. And that —"

"We don't want to leave," Laura interrupted.

"I had to tell them, Chums," Clara said softly.

"Tell them *what?*" I asked.

"Everything," she said.

She finally looked at me tentatively. Her eyes glistened with tears.

"Clara was brave enough to tell us your plan to flee to Switzerland illegally," Lieutenant Wilson said, staring daggers at me. "And your murder plot."

Murder plot?

"I studied Hegel, too, young man," Lieutenant Wilson continued. "And if you think you can use a Philosophy 101 textbook to justify murdering the executive producer of your TV show. . ."

"I don't want you to kill anyone," Clara said, fat tears

rolling down her cheeks. "They'll send you to prison. Maybe forever."

Clara had the whole thing wrong. I wasn't going to kill Brandon.

"But I wasn't planning to —" I began.

"Your sister is worried about you, Charles," Lieutenant Wilson said. "A lot of people are worried about you."

"They really are," Clara said.

"Like *who?*" I said.

"Me."

I spun around. It was Brandon. He was standing by the door.

"I'm afraid the stress of the show has really gotten to you, pal," he said, closing the door behind him.

I'd never seen Brandon in jeans before. He was wearing a diamond-stud earring above his gold hoop. His unshaven face showed the first hints of a black beard.

"He cares about you, Chums," Clara said. "He really does."

"What're you saying?" I whispered in a small voice.

"I want to go to college," Clara said.

"And I *don't* want to go to Switzerland," Laura said. "I want to be a model."

"We're working on a new line of teen clothes called

Norm," Brandon said. "We want Laura to be the spokesmodel for it. And we've made special arrangements for Clara to take the PSAT in July. We signed her up. She's all set."

"Until then," said Lieutenant Wilson, "Clara and Laura will be in protective custody."

"I'd be happy to care for them," Brandon said. "I've got plenty of room in my town house."

No!

"We've also had an offer from Sophie Buchanan," said Lieutenant Wilson. "I think the girls might be more comfortable with her. Am I right?"

"That'd be great," Clara said.

"Sophie's nice," Laura cooed.

"Protective custody?" Mom cried.

"We'll discuss visitation rights," Lieutenant Wilson said. "If the girls want to visit, that is."

I looked at Clara. With my eyes I asked: *Are you serious?*

"I want to stay, Chums," Clara said, as if reading my mind. "I really do. I want to take the PSAT. I'm working on the creative writing part now."

The door opened. Ben and Sally were escorted in to the room by the woman officer. Both were sucking on hard candy.

"At least we didn't have to get shots," Ben said sloppily, rolling the candy from one side of his mouth to the other.

In the hallway I saw the film crew. Of course they were shooting the whole thing. Of course.

*　　*　　*

It was after midnight by the time we returned to the condo — without Clara and Laura. Some Hare Krishnas in yellow robes were dancing sleepily in the lobby and chanting, "Hare Krishna, Hare Krishna, Krishna Krishna, Hare Hare."

"Weirdos," our police escort said as he led us past the group. They were burning incense.

I wondered why the concierge didn't kick them out. Then I saw a robed man sitting behind a table and the sign:

REGISTER HERE
FOR 27TH ANNUAL MEETING OF THE
INTERNATIONAL SOCIETY
OF KRISHNA CONSCIOUSNESS

The cop escorted us to the ninety-second floor. He had a key to our condo. Someone had repaired the door while we were at the police station.

"Here you go," said the officer, letting us in. "Have a nice evening."

After we filed past him, the officer stepped back in the hallway and pulled the door closed. Dad immediately started punching numbers into the door panel. Nothing. We were locked in again.

"Everybody just go to bed," Mom said.

"How can we sleep when we're being held *prisoner?*" Ben demanded with his arms outstretched.

Sally started crying.

"We'll talk about this . . . another time," Mom said. Her voice had a finality to it. It was the same voice she used when correcting math problems.

All night from my bedroom I could hear the sound of doors slamming and drawers being opened and closed. I knew it was Dad. He was pacing the condo like a wild animal locked in a cage.

My punishment from God had come full circle. Every single person in my family had been crushed because of me.

I lay awake in bed that night, paralyzed by guilt. I didn't have the energy for anger. All I could do was pray:

God, I'm sorry for all the mistakes I've made in my life. I'm sorry the stuff I write always gets me and everyone in trouble. I'm sorry I wanted to be special. I'm sorry You don't love me. But God, if You hate me so much, why don't You just kill me? Or are You waiting for me to kill myself so You can send me to hell? Because this IS hell. I am living in hell because You Won't Help Me. How could You abandon me and my family like this? Never mind. Don't answer that. I already know. It's because You hate me. Amen.

I thought for a minute. Then I added a P.S.:

I just figured it out. You're not even there, are You, God? Why do I bother talking to You and believing in You? I'm going to stop. Good-bye.

I tossed and turned for an hour before I sent up my P.P.S.:

Not that You're listening, God. You can't because You Don't Exist.

27.

Thunder woke me early on Friday morning. At six o'clock, I was standing in the living room, watching rain slap against the windows. I heard the sound of an envelope being slid under our door.

It was a note — unsigned — directing us to make a grocery list and hold it up in front of the camera in the kitchen at seven o'clock.

So they knew we knew about the hidden cameras.

We did as instructed. An hour later, armed security guards from Bargain Bonanza delivered the groceries we'd requested. Dad inspected everything — inside cereal boxes, coffee cans, a case of Cowboy Cal Kooky Cookies — for digital cameras and recording devices.

"I don't care anymore," Dad fumed after he'd peeled six bananas. "Let them see what they see."

He threw a coffee mug against the wall. Then he spent the next hour sweeping up shards of glass from the floor.

At nine o'clock, Dad was still in his robe, drinking coffee.

It rained hard all day. Sally and Ben never changed out of their pajamas. Ben was curled up in a ball at one end of the living room sofa. He was reading his pirate book. Sally sat at the other end of the sofa, watching a nature program on TV. I watched with her as a rattlesnake prepared to strike a rabbit. The rabbit was frozen in fear.

"Run, rabbit, run," Sally whispered at the TV.

Mom spent the day puttering nervously around the condo.

"Did you get some lunch, honey?" she asked me late in the afternoon. She was digging through her old sewing basket. It was one of the few things Mom'd brought with us from Normal.

"No," I mumbled.

"You should try to. . . ." Her voice trailed off tonelessly as she threaded a needle.

When I went to my bedroom, I found a note on my desk.

I'm leaving tomorrow night. Saturday. Late.
Do you want to come?

It was Dad's handwriting. I grabbed the note and a pen and crawled under my bed to write a response:

How? Is everyone going? What about C & L?

I left the note under my bed and walked to the kitchen. Dad was making another pot of coffee.

"I found your . . . shoes under my bed," I told him.

"My *what?*" he said. "Oh. Right."

Five minutes later, we passed each other in the living room. He nodded with his head in the direction of my room. I found his response on my desk. He had written it on the back of his first message.

C & L want to stay. Mom too. Free will.

My dad: the man who could fix anything. Now he was planning to destroy what I'd always thought was the most important thing in his life — our family.

I pulled Mom into my bedroom.

"I'm not going," she said before I even asked.

"But Dad is?"

"I don't know," she said faintly. "He says he can't stand this. Well? Does he think I can? But I'm not leaving without Clara and Laura. I'm not tearing this family apart. I don't know how Dad can even think of it."

"What's he thinking?" I asked.

"He keeps saying, 'Free will, free will. The girls can make their own decisions.' Clara, maybe. But Laura's nine years old. I'm not leaving my child."

Oh! I get it!

She was acting.

"I *compleeeeeetely* understand," I said, smiling maniacally. "I read you loud and clear." And then, in a whisper, I added: "You're going to win an Academy Award for this."

She looked at me blankly. "I'm dead serious, Charles. I'm not abandoning my children."

"This is really . . . *you?*" I asked.

"Of course this is me. I'm not going."

She left my room. I found Dad in the front hallway. He was holding a hammer and studying the door.

"Well?" he said. "Have you made your decision?"

I stared at Dad. His hair was sticking up in messy clumps. His eyes were bloodshot. He looked like a crazy man.

"You think I'm cracking, don't you?" Dad said, smiling.

"*What?*"

"Your mother told me about the third episode," he said. "You said I was terrible with money. You said I was cracking."

He started to laugh. It was a creepy, birdlike cackle.

"*I* didn't say that," I replied, trying to laugh, too. "Clara said she thought you were, *um* . . ."

"You told her about the tax stuff," Dad said, squinting at me. His eyes were darkly circled. He wasn't even trying to whisper.

"You must think you're pretty hot stuff to bail the old man out, eh?" he continued. "Pay off the taxes. Sign up for one of those fancy Swiss bank accounts."

Sally and Ben were watching us from the living room. Their round faces, perched on the back of the couch, looked like tiny shrunken heads.

"Dad," I said, "I was just trying to —"

"Trying to *what?*" he cut in. Sweat was pouring down his haggard face. "You want to stay here and be the *man* of the family? Fine. Because I'm out of here tomorrow night. Anybody want to come with me, come. If you want to stay and live like a bunch of animals in a zoo, stay."

"I'm going with Dad!" Ben yelled, straddling the back of the sofa.

"Now we're cooking!" Dad said victoriously. He turned and pointed to Sally.

"Are you gonna come with your old man, or stay in this hellhole and rot?"

"Frank!" Mom yelled from the other side of the living room.

"And you!" Dad bellowed. "*You* can shut up!"

He threw the hammer on the floor. Marble chips flew up in his face. He stormed down the hallway to his and Mom's bedroom.

"Mommy?" Sally said. She looked like a frightened baby animal.

"I'm going to make us some popcorn," Mom said, walking briskly to the kitchen. "Doesn't that sound good on a rainy night? We'll have popcorn for dinner. Then we'll have our baths and go to bed early."

"I'm not going to bed at *five* o'clock," Ben said.

"Is Dad leaving?" Sally asked. "Without us?"

"It's okay," Mom yelled from the kitchen. "We'll talk about this another time."

*   *   *

I was lying in bed awake at 11:32 that night when a robed figure entered my room. My heart stopped.

"Come," the figured whispered.

"No!" I gasped.

"Shhhhhh."

It was Mom. Her head was shaved. She was wearing a pale yellow sheet.

"What?" I said. My body went rigid. "No."

"Shhhhhquiet," she said, taking my hand. "Follow me."

The lights were off throughout the condo. Mom led me from my room across the living room to her and Dad's bedroom and then into their master bathroom. My eyes slowly adjusted to the vision in front of me.

Dad was sitting on the edge of the bathtub. He was wearing a sheet like Mom's. His head was also shaved. He was using an electric razor to shear the hair from Sally's head.

"It'll grow back," Sally whispered to me. I could tell from her quivering voice that she'd been crying.

Mom was pulling a yellow sheet over Ben's bald head.

"Isn't this *soooo* cool?" Ben mouthed to me.

I nodded.

I knelt while Dad shaved my head. The razor's tiny red ON indicator was the only light in the room, the soft *hummmbuzz* the only noise. I could feel the vibration behind my eyes.

"What about —?" I started to ask.

"It's okay," Dad whispered.

Mom gave me a sheet with a circle cut in the center. I slipped the sheet over my head. Then Mom handed me a long piece of rope. I tied it around my waist like the others had. She placed a small pouch in my hand. It was made of the same yellow sheet material.

"We can't take much," Mom said softly. "Just what you can fit in here. And take your watch. The Little Benny."

Sally was filling her pouch with plastic animals and a rosary. Ben was stuffing his with old pirate eye patches and a lucky buckeye he'd had since Normal.

"Hands and knees," Mom said. She pointed to the floor.

So I crawled on my knees back to my bedroom. I grabbed a pen and started to look for paper. I needed to leave a note for people to find. I wanted to tell the whole story. But there was no time.

"Come on, Charles," Dad whispered.

He was in my bedroom doorway, hunched over on his hands and knees. The others were following behind in a single-file line. Together we crawled down the front hall.

Dad opened the door effortlessly. We stood and tiptoed to the elevator. We were barefoot.

"You look funny," Sally giggled, pointing at my head.

"We all look funny," Dad whispered.

Mom and Dad led us through the lobby of El Rancho, past a group of dozing Hare Krishnas, and into the street. Two empty limos were waiting for us. The engines were running, but there were no drivers.

Dad directed me to sit next to him, in the front seat of the first limo. Sally climbed in the backseat. Mom took Ben to the second limo.

"We're leaving without Laura and Clara?" I asked.

"Of course not," Dad said.

He handed me a note.

Meet us Friday at midnight. Charles will know where.

It was Clara's handwriting. I looked at the digital clock on the limo's dashboard: 11:51. We were pulling away from El Rancho.

"Okay, where do we meet them?" Dad asked. He was watching Mom in the rearview mirror pull behind him in the second limo.

I could feel my heartbeat in my newly bald head.

"I'm thirsty," Sally said from the backseat.

"I know, sweetheart," Dad said. "We'll get something to

drink in a little while." His voice dropped. "Charles, tell me where to go."

It was 11:52. My mind was a blur. I hadn't spoken with Clara since the police station. I had no idea where we'd meet.

"She said you'd know," Dad said.

My chest tightened. I felt the old familiar nausea of being pushed too high on a swing set.

"Where'd that note come from?" I asked.

"She slipped it to Mom at the police station," Dad said. "Charles, she was *acting.*"

My mind flashed back to the last thing Clara had said to me: *I'm working on the creative writing part now.*

Oh!

"Straight ahead," I said.

I knew exactly where we'd meet at midnight.

28.

Clara and Laura were waiting for us in the cemetery, next to Leona and Little James's grave. Mom waved the girls over to her limo.

Dad led the convoy of two for almost four hours. He drove fast and recklessly, checking the rearview mirror constantly to make sure Mom was behind us. I had a million questions, but said nothing.

It was still dark when we pulled onto the shoulder of Highway 965. Dad engaged the parking brake.

"Everybody out on my side," he said.

Sally and I piled out while Mom pulled her limo in behind us. Ben and Laura tumbled out sleepily. Clara crawled out after Mom. I noticed that Clara's eyes were fixed on something on the other side of the limo.

That's when I saw the cliff.

"I need everybody's watches," Mom said, sliding hers off her wrist.

My brother and sisters silently pulled their Little Benny watches from their pouches and wrists.

"Charles, your watch," Mom said.

I was still staring at the jagged rock formation beneath us.

"I need your watch," Mom said.

I gave it to her. She carefully placed it and the rest of my family's watches in Dad's limo.

Dad was in a nearby grassy area. He was picking up rocks and discarding them. Minutes later, he came back to the limos, carrying a stone the size of a ham. He untied the rope from his waist and pulled the sheet over his head. His chest was bare. He was wearing his old cutoff shorts.

"Charles, hold this," Dad directed.

I took the sheet from him and watched as he used his rope to tie the stone to the accelerator pedal in his limo.

"Everybody in Mom's car," Dad said.

We followed his instructions. I sat in the backseat, next to Clara. She was holding our passports. Mom put her limo in reverse. The passenger door to the front seat was still open.

"Wait!" Sally yelled. "We hafta close the door."

"We can't leave without Dad!" Ben hollered.

"Please, I need quiet," Mom said. Her eyes were on Dad.

"Back, back," Dad said, motioning with his hands.

He was standing next to the limo he'd driven. And then, slowly, with the precision that comes from practicing something a million times in your head, he released the parking brake as he pushed the gearshift into drive. He jumped back from the moving limo.

"Go!" Dad yelled to Mom as he dove into the passenger side of her limo and pulled the door closed behind him.

We watched in awe as Dad's limo, now empty except for our Little Benny watches, soared over the cliff.

*   *   *

Weeks later, after we were settled in Mexico, I tracked down our obituary on the Internet at the local library.

The Harrisongs: Dead!

From Houseboat to Household Name, America's Normal *Family Perishes in Freak Crash*

(FREDERICKSBURG, TX) Seven members of the Harrisong family, stars of Bargain Bonanza's popular Real-vertising campaign, were pronounced dead early yesterday morning.

Though the cause of death is still under investigation, authorities agree that a limousine stolen by the family plunged off a 400-foot cliff on Highway 965, near Enchanted Rock State Natural Area, north of Fredericksburg.

Killed in the crash were Frank and Allison

Harrisong, along with their five children: Clara, Charles, Ben, Laura, and Sally.

The Harrisongs, originally from Normal, Illinois, were selected last year by Bargain Bonanza to be the discount giant's spokesfamily. The Harrisongs helped Bargain Bonanza launch the NormalWear brand of clothing and lifestyle products and were the inspiration for the top-rated TV show, *The Harrisongs: Live!*

Ironically, the family's fame may have contributed to their deaths.

Several television stations in the Dallas metro area received what appear to be suicide letters written by the Harrisongs.

"We can no longer live like this," the family said in handwritten letters sent to the media before their death. "We respect Bargain Bonanza's legal claims on our right of publicity, but we also feel that we have the right to live as human beings. As the philosopher Hegel once said, the only way a conflict between right and right can end is with the death of one side or the other. And so, good-bye."

The letters included a list of abuses the Harrisongs claim they were subjected to by Bargain Bonanza and a plea to the networks to air a video the family taped while living in a penthouse condo in downtown Dallas.

Attorneys for Bargain Bonanza say the tape is corporate property and they have no plans to broadcast it at this time.

Company spokesperson Lawrence Leech also said he disputes the suicide theory.

"The Harrisongs had a criminal history that predated their work with us," said Leech at a press conference held yesterday afternoon outside the New York Stock Exchange. "When we discovered the Harrisongs' criminal past, which included tax evasion and inappropriate familial relations, we felt compelled to tell authorities with the Dallas Police Department and the Texas Department of Family and Protective Services."

Leech refused to say if he was accusing the Harrisongs of fleeing from authorities.

"It's regrettable that all seven members of the Harrisong family were killed in the accident," Leech said, reading from a prepared statement. "But you have to ask yourself: Where were they driving in the middle of the night? What were they running from? An innocent man doesn't run. Nor does a normal family."

News of the Harrisongs' deaths triggered a 94 percent drop in Bargain Bonanza stock yesterday. Additional losses are possible if media outlets are successful in their effort to get a court order to compel Bargain Bonanza to broadcast the Harrisongs' self-produced video.

While some corporate analysts suggest that Bargain Bonanza has already begun a campaign to distance itself from the Harrisongs, Charles Goodman, the founder of Bargain Bonanza, said he did not regret the choice of the Harrisongs to represent the discount giant as its first spokes-family.

"There was something about the family that captured my heart and that of America," said Goodman from his home in Alabama. "They will not be forgotten."

Goodman amassed a multibillion fortune from a chain of discount pharmacies he started in Geneva, Illinois. He founded Bargain Bonanza a decade ago, but retired soon thereafter so he could pursue his hobbies: publishing and star hunting.

Funeral services are pending for the Harrisongs, whose bodies were incinerated in the fiery crash north of the pink granite exfoliation dome known as Enchanted Rock. The site is not far from where Frank Harrisong and young Ben filmed a Bargain Bonanza commercial last year.

All that remained in the charred wreckage were the family's engraved watches from Bargain Bonanza's Little Benny line of waterproof, fireproof timepieces.

"You have to admit that's quite impressive," Lawrence Leech said at the press conference. "The durability of Little Benny watches is the real take-away message here."

Leech ended the press conference by reminding investors that Little Benny watches are available in Bargain Bonanza stores worldwide, excluding Latin America.

"Who wrote the suicide note?" I asked Dad one afternoon. I was still trying to piece the whole story together.

"Clara," Dad said. "Pretty good, eh? We were all pretty darn good, I'd say. Hey, I think I'm going to pierce my ear like Brandon."

"No, you're not," Mom said. She was sitting in the shade, quizzing Sally on her Spanish spelling words.

"But I'd look good with an earring," Dad said.

Mom laughed. "Be quiet and fix the toilet."

When we found the rental casita near Merida, Mexico, Dad had joked that the house had a Harrisong toilet.

"It's always running," he said.

My family. We were turning into a vaudeville act.

"I liked it when I pretended I wanted to be a model," Laura said. "I was a good actress, wasn't I?"

"Remember when I pulled that catnip mouse out of the Cowboy Cal One-Mix Campfire DinnerFix and pretended it was a real mouse?" Ben reminisced. "That was *sooooo* funny. I liked being able to play me."

The first month we were in Mexico, Laura and Ben spent most mornings stretched out in hammocks on the porch, working on long-division problems while Dad and I put a new roof on our yellow casita.

Mom didn't like talking about the escape. The only thing she ever told me was that she and Dad began discussing how we had to leave Dallas the night after that first Brand Identity meeting, when we were shown the creepy *Meet the Harrisongs!* report.

Dad loved talking about our exodus in detail: how he'd broken the door lock with tools he made from silverware. How he'd hotwired both limos. How he found that aluminum rowboat in a weedy marsh outside Corpus Christi. How he ditched the limousine in the water and rowed us through the night to Mexico.

"I got us into that mess with Bargain Bonanza," Dad

told me one afternoon when we were finishing the roof. "It was my job to get us out of it."

Before I could correct him, he laughed and added: "Besides, I had to reestablish my role as the leading man in this family. Well, until I turn fifty, anyway. Then you or Ben can take over."

"I'll be the hero then!" Ben yelled up from the porch. "Dad, remember it was my idea to fake that we died."

"*Your* idea," I hollered down.

It was *my* idea. Well, it was Hegel's idea. But it was my idea to steal Hegel's idea.

"That's how they caught Edward Teach," Ben shouted. "He thought Lieutenant Robert Maynard's crew was dead. So Teach and his fellow pirates boarded the navy sloop. But Maynard's guys weren't dead. They were faking it. They were hiding below. Maynard and his guys tricked Edward Teach, the meanest pirate who ever lived. And then they killed him and the reign of fear was over."

"How come I've never heard of this Edward Teach guy?" Dad asked, leaning over the roof.

"You probably know him by his nickname," Ben yelled. "Blackbeard. But his real name was Edward Teach. His ship was called *Adventure*."

When did Ben get so smart?

"Charles," Dad said quietly.

"Yeah?"

"I hope I didn't scare you with that crazy man stuff," he said. "Yelling at you and Mom on that last day in the condo."

"No," I lied. "I wasn't scared."

"I had to do that," Dad explained. "Just in case Brandon was watching us on the surveillance cameras. I had to make him think we were leaving the next night. I had to beat those guys at their own game."

"I know," I said.

I didn't have the heart to tell my dad how Bargain Bonanza had used even our deaths to make a buck off their crummy Little Benny watches.

* * *

A week later, Dad decided the view from the roof of our casita was too pretty to waste. Plus, it was cooler on the roof at night.

So Dad built a plywood sleeping porch on top of the casita. We bought sleeping bags at the local market and dragged them up by ladder.

"In the old days, sailors navigated by the stars," Ben said the first night we all slept on the roof. "Before they had maps, they used the stars."

"Who told you that?" I asked.

"I read it in my pirate book," Ben said. He squirmed out of his sleeping bag and propped himself on both elbows. "Charles, I'm not *retarded,* you know."

"I know," I said.

"We should learn how to do that," Dad said. "I'll see if I can find a star book. We'll learn all the constellations."

"Hey, do you guys know what *disaster* means in Greek?" Sally asked. "It was in my trivia book. Guess."

"I think it means . . . a plane crash," said Laura, half dozing.

"*Disaster* doesn't mean plane crash," Ben said. "It means . . . um, what's it mean, Mom?"

"Hmmm, let's think," Mom said. "In Greek, *dis* means *not.* Or maybe *un* or *bad.* And *aster* is —"

"A flower?" said Clara.

"It means *bad star,*" Sally said impatiently.

Bad star. Maybe that's what I'd seen in Mr. Goodman's telescope. Maybe that's what I was: a bad star.

"The sun's the biggest star," Ben said. "Just in case anybody didn't know that."

"*Everybody* knows that," Laura said, sitting up in her sleeping bag.

"Now that I've *told* you, you know," Ben said. "But you didn't know before —"

"Shhhhhh," Mom said gently. "It's late. Let's everybody settle down. Think quiet thoughts to yourself."

I listened to the sounds of my family fade, replaced by the clatter of noisy parrots roosting in nearby trees. My eyes slowly panned the scene of all of us lying under the indigo sky, like a crew of landlocked sailors. It amused me to think that, for the first time, we really *did* look like a TV family: the Swiss Family Harrisongs, safe in our very own home-made penthouse suite.

Not that we were in Switzerland, of course. And not that I'd ever withdraw money from that Swiss bank account. (Why risk letting anyone, even a banker in Switzerland, know we were still alive?)

But there was a quiet, authentic drama to our new lives in Mexico. And finally, not a television camera in sight to film it.

Maybe we really were bad stars. We were certainly terrible at being celebrities. But we weren't the lousy actors I thought we were. And nobody played us better than us.

Charles Goodman was right: You have to wait till dark to see the stars, even though they're always there.

29.

It took a long time for our hair to grow out. When it finally did, Sally never chewed hers again.

She lost her speech impediment, too. In fact, Sally was the only one in the family who ever learned to roll her *R*s when speaking Spanish. Dad sometimes took her along on jobs to be his translator.

Without even trying, Dad created a bustling business, thanks to our rooftop sleeping porch. First our neighbors began asking him to build porches on their roofs. Pretty soon, people were driving more than a hundred miles to see if Dad would build rooftop sleeping porches for them.

He did. He also hired a bookkeeper.

Mom resumed her homeschooling duties. Clara started taking private art lessons at a local studio. She painted portraits for a few of Dad's wealthier clients. She still had no interest in school ("Sitting in a classroom just isn't who I *am*"), and Mom and Dad didn't force the issue.

"I passed my PSAT by writing those suicide letters," Clara said. "And, please, I knew what the plan was all along — as if Chums could ever *kill* anybody."

It was a month after we arrived in Mexico that Clara finally told me about Sophie.

"She wanted me to give you something," Clara said.

"I'm not interested," I said.

Clara and I were taking one of our nightly walks around the neighborhood. The locals no longer stared, but simply lifted their chins and smiled. A pack of wild dogs raced past us.

"Chums," Clara said, "she helped."

"Who?"

"Sophie," said Clara. "She drove Laura and me to the cemetery that night."

"*What?*"

"And she arranged for that rowboat to be in Corpus Christi. Here. Just read this."

Clara handed me a sealed envelope and walked home. I sat on a park bench and read the letter as dogs fought in the distance:

Dear Charles,

I'm glad I got to spend one more night with Clara and Laura. It gave me a chance to apologize to them for screwing up in New York. I wish I could've apologized to you in person, but it just didn't work out that way.

I'm so sorry about everything. I never meant to hurt you or your family. I liked you guys from the moment I saw you. And I'm sorry I lied about having a son. I don't know why I said that. I was just trying to make you feel better that day you were sick in the bathroom. It was a stupid thing to say.

Now if you promise not to roll your eyes (which you DO, you know), I'll tell you something: When we were talking in the bathroom that day, do you know what I was thinking? I'll tell you. I thought, What a nice kid. I wish I had a son like that.

(I'm not lying. It's true.)

Anyway, I'm going to India. Not sure exactly where or even why. But I need a new start, too.

I hope we both find what we're looking for.

With love,

Sophie

A nice kid, huh?

A son.

Oh well. At least she signed it *With love.* That meant something, right?

*   *   *

You might say as America fell in love with my family, I fell in love with Sophie Buchanan. And like many loves, both were based on hope and misplaced ideals.

I don't know if my family was good for America, but I think Sophie was good for me. She taught me things you can't learn from a book, like the fact that we see what we need to see in people, and the rest we ignore — until the stuff we're ignoring becomes bigger than the stuff we made up to talk ourselves into love in the first place.

But she also taught me how fun it is to feel those crazy, loopy feelings about someone. It gives you something new to think about it. It makes you interested enough in life to keep going. Because you've got to keep going. Or at least I do. In the immortal words of Cowboy Chaz, *I gotta go.*

*   *   *

In July, Clara planned a surprise party for my fifteenth birthday. It was at midnight. Sally woke me up by tickling me. I almost fell off the roof.

I opened my gifts in the moonlight. Dad had made me a leather tool belt. Mom gave me a pillow she'd made from feathers she got at the local market. Sally gave me some papayas she'd picked. Laura gave me a necklace of flowers and weeds she'd found around our casita. Ben presented me with a gift certificate to *borrow* one of his pirate eye patches.

Clara painted my portrait on a piece of driftwood. She also gave me a package of blank paper. Even in the dark, I could see the tire marks on it.

"I found it in the street yesterday," Clara apologized. "But it's good enough, isn't it? For writing? You should write your own philosophy book, Chums. Or write a mystery — or a book about this whole year. Write it all."

(You'd think I'd learn my lesson, wouldn't you?)

Here's the funny part. Of all the stuff that happened that year, the thing I remember most isn't the day I spent filming that stupid laxative commercial. Or all the hours I sat in those never-ending Brand Identity meetings. It's not even "Blackbeard Brandon," as we later nicknamed him.

It's the way those stone lions, Patience and Fortitude, sit in front of the New York Public Library. So close to each other, but never able to touch. Never able even to look at each other. They just stare straight ahead, day and night.

Maybe they're mad at each other. Maybe one lion betrayed the other, and that's why they don't talk. Or maybe it's because what they have to say goes beyond words.

This isn't what I thought when I first saw the stone lions in New York. Back then, I just thought how funny and wonderful they were. Giant guard kitties in front of a library! I couldn't resist waving at them. I was giddy with a happiness that made me want to connect with everyone and everything in sight.

The point is, when I saw the lions for the first time, I was in love with Sophie Buchanan. And I had the weirdest feeling that maybe she loved me a little, too. The dull ordinariness of *me* had been replaced with the extraordinary possibility of *us*.

If someone had asked me right then, as I stood in front of the New York Public Library, *Do you know thyself?*, I would've answered with a triumphant *Yes! I am a person in love with Sophie!* And no matter what happened later, for that one moment, the world burned brighter. *I* burned brighter, like a hot white star piercing through the night sky.

Love. It's what takes you far from normal. It's what shakes you from your unadventurous orbit, your dull little plan. It plucks you from the crowd and makes you feel wonderful; makes you believe this Earth really is an enchanted rock.

Of course love can also make you feel like a freakin' idiot. It depends on how you look at love — as a punishment or a gift. Everything depends on how you think and what you believe.

Even Charles Goodman. You could say our Bargain Bonanza nightmare was his fault. Or you could believe he's the man who saved our lives. After all, it was the $1,200 he gave me that paid the first three months' rent on our casita in Mexico. That money was the only thing I took from the condo in Dallas, besides my Little Benny watch, a pen, and the shell keychain to the S.S. *O'Migosh* my dad made for me.

Because you've always got to save something for the next adventure. There's always another, better adventure up ahead. You just have to believe that and keep going — even if you don't know where or why or how.

Run, rabbit, run.

That, I've decided, is what I believe. I guess you could call it my philosophy — or my prayer.

God, You have an interesting style and a real flair for the dramatic.

Case in point: Thanks to Clara, according to my passport, I'm now George Harrison.

I'm also almost out of paper, so I'll end by just saying this: There are doves in Mexico. Thousands of them. I think of Brandon every time I see those nice white birds. I wonder how he knew, if he knew.

I wonder if anybody really knows anything.

After a year of studying philosophy, the only thing I know for sure is that I don't know anything at all — except for the obvious: I believe in things I don't understand.

I believe in mysteries.

And I believe an innocent man does run — must run — not from his past, but toward the unimaginable adventure that lies ahead.